NO ONE
TO TRUST

MELODY CARLSON

D0311110

❖ **HARLEQUIN** LOVE INSPIRED® SUSPENSE

Recycling programs
for this product may
not exist in your area.

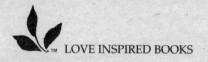 LOVE INSPIRED BOOKS

ISBN-13: 978-0-373-44726-8

No One to Trust

www.Harlequin.com

Printed in U.S.A.

The guy had a gun trained on the woman Jon had seen earlier.

"Call off that dog!" the man screamed at Jon.

"Come here, boy," Jon said with authority. His tail between his legs, Ralph slowly approached and Jon scooped him up. The little dog's body was tense, as if on high alert, as if something was still very wrong.

"Now get outta here!" the guy yelled, waving his weapon.

The frightened woman watched Jon with a tear-streaked face. He knew he needed to do something—but what?

"I warned you!" The man looked flustered and agitated—as if trying to make up his mind. Probably deciding which one of them to shoot next.

In that same split second, Jon looked at the woman and made his decision. *"Run!"* he yelled at her.

As the man with the gun turned to the woman, Jon sprang at him and knocked him flat onto the graveled road, making the revolver fly from his hand.

"Run for your life!" Jon yelled at her.

Melody Carlson has worn many hats, from preschool teacher to political activist to senior editor. But most of all, she loves to write! She has published over two hundred books—with sales of over six million copies, and she has received the *RT Book Reviews* Lifetime Achievement Award. She and her husband have two grown sons and live in Sisters, Oregon, with their Labrador retriever, Audrey. They enjoy skiing, hiking and biking in the Cascade Mountains.

Books by Melody Carlson

Love Inspired Suspense

Perfect Alibi
No One to Trust

Trust in the Lord with all your heart,
and don't depend on your own understanding.
Remember the Lord in all you do,
and He will give you success.
—*Proverbs* 3:5-6

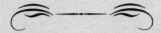

ONE

Jon Wilson hoped to see her again today—the runner who'd caught his eye on the beach almost a week ago. The woman he'd been looking for every day ever since. But by the time he and his dog, Ralph, made it to that section of beach, it was late in the afternoon and the fog was rolling in. Not likely she'd be out for a run now. Why hadn't he stopped painting a couple of hours ago?

Ready to turn back, Jon wanted to kick himself for not getting her name when he'd had the chance. Instead, he'd tried to appear like the "responsible pet owner" by scolding Ralph for chasing after her. Even though she'd seemed to enjoy the silly dog romping alongside her. And Ralph, fully enamored with the pretty blonde with the sunny smile and swinging ponytail, had acted as if he were her new best friend. Too bad Jon hadn't taken Ralph's "hint" and befriended her himself. Now it was probably too late. At least for today. Jon glanced down at his ensemble and chuckled. Perhaps it was for the best. In his hurry to get down here, he still had on his old paint-smeared flannel shirt over a faded T-shirt and raggedy cargo pants, also paint-smeared. Even his shaggy hair was overdue for a haircut. Not exactly dressed to impress.

As he called Ralph to go home, a siren sounded. The loud shrill blast was cut short, as if in warning, but it seemed to originate in the small parking area where the beach road ended at the foot of the dunes. The same place he'd suspected the runner might've parked her car when she'd come to run the other day. And the same reason he'd been walking down this far once or twice a day. Hoping to "casually" meet her again. With Ralph's help, of course.

Curious as to what was up, Jon was just considering investigating when Ralph decided to take action. Giving out a sharp bark, he took off, racing toward the dunes that bordered the road. Jon thought about calling him back but, well aware of how his mother's stubborn terrier took orders, he knew it was pointless. Besides, it might be important to know what was going on. His parents, who visited their beach cabin fairly regularly, had mentioned various rumors of criminal activity in these parts. Both retired attorneys, they had their different theories about what was actually going on. His dad seemed to think it was nothing, but his mom was suspiciously wary. Maybe Jon would discover a new piece of the puzzle for them. Besides, he needed to get Ralph.

Leah Hampton felt her stomach knot as she watched the uniformed officer from her rearview mirror. His plump face appeared flushed and slightly irritated in the late-afternoon sun. Glancing around the deserted dune area, as if worried someone else was around, he adjusted his dark glasses and sauntered up to her old Subaru. She'd noticed the unmarked car several miles back but hadn't been concerned. She hadn't been speeding on this isolated stretch of beach road—her car's worn shocks couldn't take it.

A wave of fresh anxiety swept over Leah as she reached for her wallet, ready to fish out her driver's license and insurance card. She hoped her car's registration hadn't expired or that a taillight hadn't burnt out. Those infractions could result in fines—expenses she couldn't afford right now. She remembered the last time she'd been pulled over several years ago and how she'd talked her way out of a ticket. But she'd been dressed to the nines that night. Not so today.

Getting out of her car, she adjusted her running tank and smoothed her running shorts, forcing an optimistic smile. "Hello," she said in a friendly tone. "I was just heading out for a beach run. Is something wrong, Officer?"

"Is that your car?"

"Yep." She nodded at her old beater. "And I know I wasn't speeding."

"No…." He slowly glanced over his shoulder again. What was he looking for? "You weren't speeding."

"So what's up?" She looked around, too. "Is there some kind of danger out here? I mean I do get a little concerned about jogging alone this time of day, especially down here, where there's no phone connectivity. But I love this part of the beach, and I'm training for the Portland marathon and it's hard to get my running time in." She smiled again, deciding to try the sympathy card as she rambled on. "You see, I work part time at The Willows and—"

"You'll need to come with me," he said abruptly.

"Come with you?" She stared into the lenses of his dark sunglasses, trying to see the eyes behind them, but only the double image of her own puzzled face reflected back at her. *"Why?"*

"Because I have a warrant for your arrest."

"But I haven't *done* anything—I haven't broken any laws."

"Turn around."

"But you haven't even checked my ID. You don't know who I am." She held up her wallet, but before she could remove her driver's license, he smacked her hand, sending the wallet spilling to the ground.

"Doesn't matter who you are," he growled, "not where you're going."

A silent alarm went off inside her. Something was seriously wrong here. This cop—if he was really a cop—was dangerous.

"I, uh, I think you've mistaken me for someone else," she said in a shaky voice, slowly stepping away from him, hoping to jump into her car and attempt a getaway or at least lean into her horn to get attention from a passerby. Not that there were any. Instead she bumped into the car door, slamming it shut with a loud bang.

In the same instant, he lunged toward her, grabbing her bare upper arm in a viselike grip. "I suggest you come quietly, blondie."

"But I haven't done anything to—"

"Look, we can do this the easy way or the *hard way.*" He was so close she could feel his hot breath in her face. His pudgy lips curled slightly, sending a wave of nausea through her.

"You've got the wrong—"

"Okay!" He flipped her around to face her car with one arm twisted painfully behind her back. "You wanna do this the hard way. Fine by me." He chuckled in a creepy way. "Just you wait and see, blondie." He pinned her tightly against her car. As he fumbled with his handcuffs, short puffs of hot breath went down the back of her neck.

Her mind racing, Leah knew she was in trouble. Serious trouble. This guy was obviously not a cop. Or if he was a cop, he was a crooked one!

"Let me go!" she screamed at him, hoping to get the attention of a passerby. Although her hope of there being another human in the vicinity was fast fading. "You don't even know who I am. And I tell you, *I'm innocent*!" He continued to ignore her and, roughly pressing the side of her face into the gritty roof of her car, he attempted to latch a cuff around her flailing wrist.

"Shut up and stop squirming!" he growled into her ear, unable to get control of her writhing hands.

"I didn't do anything!" she screamed. "You've got the wrong person—just let me explain! I'm innocent! You've made a mis—"

Her words were cut off by a barking dog. She tried to turn to see, but the cop, still wrestling with the handcuffs, kept her pinned so tightly that she felt her ribs were about to crack. The cop cursed at the dog, tell-

ing him to "beat it or else!" but the dog kept on barking—almost as if it knew she was in trouble, and was
trying to help.

Jon knew something was amiss as soon as he came
over the ridge of the dunes. The way the unmarked car
had boxed in the old Subaru, the way the uniformed
cop had the girl pinned too roughly against her car.
The creep factor was high. But when Jon glimpsed the
woman's profile, his hackles went up. It was the girl
from the other day. Only now her expression was seriously frightened and she was yelling out that she was
innocent. "You're arresting me without just cause," she
shouted. "You're not a real cop."

"What's going on here?" Jon called out over Ralph's
noisy barking.

The cop turned to Jon with a surprised expression.

"Can I be of help?" Jon continued ambling down the
dune, trying to act natural.

"Yeah! Get that stupid mutt outta here!" the cop
yelled. *"Now!"*

Jon called to Ralph as he slowly moved closer to the
unsettling scene. Naturally the dog did not respond. Jon
hadn't expected him to.

"Call off your dog—*right now*!" the cop yelled angrily. *"Or else!"*

"Back off, Ralph!" Jon commanded and, to his
amazement, the little terrier quieted some.

"And you stay right there!" the cop told Jon. *"I mean
it!"*

"Fine." Jon stopped in his tracks, reminding himself

to go easy. Was this guy an imposter like the woman suggested? As he tried to gauge the situation, he wished he hadn't left his cell phone behind. Even without connectivity, he could be gathering valuable video.

"What's the problem, Officer?" Jon kept his voice calm and respectful.

"Police business. Now get your mutt and yourself outta here!" he yelled.

Of course, his loud voice set Ralph to barking all over again. Appreciating this distraction, Jon moved closer to the scene. "Don't worry." He tried to sound casual. "His bark is worse than his bite. Well, actually he's never bitten anyone."

"Stay right where you are!" The cop stepped away from the girl, still holding tightly to her arm, but now she was able to stand up straight. She looked at Jon with desperate brown eyes but didn't say a word.

"Just trying to get my dog." Jon held up his hands, forcing an uneasy smile. "Like you said to."

"Freeze, *right there!*" the cop shouted, setting Ralph to barking louder. "And control your dog or *I will.*"

Jon wanted to question how he was supposed to control Ralph if the cop wouldn't let him move. Instead, he took a different approach. "So what's going on here?" he asked in a friendly tone, keeping his eyes on the helpless girl who didn't look as if she could hurt a fly.

"None of your—"

"He says there's a warrant on me," the girl shouted, "but I've never done anything illegal—*ever*! And he won't even check my ID—and he hasn't read my Miranda rights—he's a fake and—"

"Shut up!" The cop glanced over his shoulder at her, then back at Jon. He seemed to be rattled as he turned to fully face Jon. "I told you to get that stupid mutt outta here!"

"I would have to *move* to get the dog," Jon explained. "You told me to freeze."

Suddenly the cop released his hold on the girl and reached for his holster, removing his revolver. *"Now! I mean it—or else!"*

"Come here, Ralph," Jon said with authority. His tail between his legs, Ralph slowly approached, and Jon scooped him up. The little dog's body was tense, as if on high alert, as if something were still very wrong.

"Now get outta here!" The cop brandished his weapon.

"Unarmed here," Jon held up one hand, holding Ralph with the other.

The cop cursed, and pointed the weapon at him.

Before he could stop him, Ralph sprang from Jon's arms and returned to barking. The frightened woman, free from the cop's grasp now, watched Jon with a tear-streaked face. He knew he needed to do something—but what? His training and experience as an attorney suggested he should attempt to talk him down.

"I can see something is wrong," Jon suggested in a calm but firm tone, "but maybe we can discuss this in a civilized manner." He considered informing the cop that he was an attorney. He could express interest in this woman's rights, offer to be her legal representation. "I'd like to suggest—"

"I already told you what to do—get your stupid mutt

and get outta here!" Despite his angry tone, the cop looked uncertain. He was clearly caught off guard by this uncomfortable triangle—a woman behind him, Jon about thirty feet in the opposite direction and a little dog barking several feet away.

"I warned you!" The cop aimed his gun at Ralph.

"Stop!" Jon lunged for the dog as a loud bang sliced the air. Ralph let out a yelp, collapsing to the ground. The woman screamed, and Jon, frozen in place, felt his adrenaline boiling. His eyes fixed on the cop, he weighed the situation. This cop, if he was one, was definitely crooked. But he was also armed. And dangerous.

The cop looked flustered and agitated—as if trying to make up his mind. Probably deciding which one of them to shoot next. In that same split second, Jon knew without a doubt that this cop was either an imposter or dirty. He looked at the woman and made his decision. *"Run!"* he yelled at her.

As the cop turned to the girl, Jon sprang at him. Making a huge leap, he blindsided the distracted man. Although the cop was much stouter, Jon's momentum knocked him flat onto the graveled road, making the revolver fly from his hand.

But the woman was still standing there!

"Run for your life!" Jon yelled at her. He could tell he'd knocked the wind out of the startled cop, but every second was precious. *"Run!"* he shouted. But instead of fleeing, she sprinted straight toward them and snatched up Ralph. Then she turned and, like a shot, she flew up the side of the dune.

TWO

The red-faced cop cursed angrily when he regained his breath. *"You're a dead man!"* he growled as he swung a fist at Jon. As Jon dodged the blow, he noticed the service revolver just a few feet away and reached for it. At the same moment, the cop went for it, too, and both men scrambled in the sand and gravel, fighting for the weapon. The cop swung another massive fist, and as Jon dodged he was able to solidly kick the revolver, sending it spinning into the nearby brush. As the cop leaped for his gun, Jon sprinted up the side of the tall dune.

Just seconds from the beach grass on top, Jon heard the first shot. Kicking it into high gear, he raced for the top just as several shots cracked in quick succession. As he dove for the cover of the grass, he felt a searing jolt on the outer side of his right thigh. He'd been hit. Ducking down, he crawled on all fours, using the tall grass to conceal himself as a couple more shots flew past. He knew that, despite the pain in his thigh, he had to keep moving. *Fast!*

Crouching low, Jon crawled to the other side of the

dune, then continued to run. He had no doubt the cop was following—or that he wanted him dead. Because dead men don't talk. Jon's only hope was that, despite his throbbing leg, he could outrun the overweight man. If he was a real cop, which seemed unlikely. And if he was a real cop, he wouldn't be one for long. Because Jon intended to turn the jerk in, as soon as he got the chance. That is if the cop didn't kill him first.

As Jon pressed on through the dunes, he prayed that the woman had taken his nonverbal hint and headed north. Cabins, including his parents' place, were in that direction. And even though most of the vacation cabins sat vacant this time of the year, there was a better chance of her finding help up there. In the meantime, he was determined to lead the crooked cop away from her by heading south. He knew this stretch of shoreline was void of civilization for the next several miles—all the way to the jetty. He also knew that if his body gave out—and that seemed likely—he would probably be dead before sundown.

Leah paused to catch her breath and, hearing the dog's pathetic whines, looked down. Seeing the hurt confusion in his golden eyes, she spoke quietly to him as she paused to examine his gunshot wound. She knew from the day they'd met on the beach that his name was Ralph. His master's name was still a mystery.

"It's okay, Ralphie," she said quietly as she checked his left hindquarter. Although it was bleeding, she was relieved to see the bullet had only grazed him. "You're going to be okay, little guy," she said soothingly. "We can fix that up." Still, she knew from her nurse's training that direct pressure was needed to stop the bleeding.

With nothing to use as a bandage, she decided to turn his wounded side toward her midsection. If she could hold him tightly against herself, she might be able to slow down or stop the bleeding. Knowing it was the best she could do and there was no time to waste, she took off running again.

As badly as she felt for the man who had come to her aid—Ralph's master—she knew that all she could do at this point was to run for her life, as he'd urged her to do. But the memory of those gunshots—after she'd run—was still reverberating through her. What if he'd been killed?

With no time to think about this, she focused on getting herself and Ralph out of harm's way. If that were even possible. And as she sprinted through the beach grass, she silently prayed for Ralph's owner. Unless she'd imagined it, the stranger's eyes had suggested a northward direction, but she had gone the opposite way. Intentionally. Her plan was to cut through the creek and double back in the surf, in an effort to hide her footprints.

After Jon had gone about half a mile, he knew he needed to tend his wound. Besides the pain, which had subsided some, he knew he was leaving a trail of blood. Fortunately the old plaid flannel shirt he was wearing over his T-shirt could help. He removed it and wrapped it tightly around his thigh, using the sleeves to secure it. If the cop was trailing him—and that was preferable to the man tracking down the woman—he could at least attempt to make it more difficult. And the longer it took the cop to find Jon, the better the chances for the pretty brown-eyed lady—who he hoped was headed in the opposite direction.

The memory of the slender woman dressed in her running clothes shoved roughly against her car by the heavyset cop filled Jon with a fresh sense of outrage. And with his bandage secured, that anger propelled him even faster. Everything about the scene had felt wrong. All wrong. Even if the girl was a wanted felon, which he seriously doubted, the cop had been inappropriately rough. Not to mention *inappropriate*. Plus he'd broken the law by not reading the girl her Miranda rights or checking her ID. There had been lots of red flags—strong implications that the cop was not on the up-and-up. He remembered his mother's opinions about the local law enforcement. "Most of them are very good, but there are a few bad apples that spoil everything."

He really hoped that creep was on his trail right now—and not following the woman. She was obviously kind and sweet and good—she'd taken care to pick up the injured dog. He prayed she was safe—and Ralph, too.

Jon's plan was to head south until he reached a run-off creek that would conceal his footprints as he turned toward the ocean. And then, with the help of the fog to hide him, he would double back in the surf, erasing his footprints all the way back up the beach. But when he reached the place where the creek trickled through the bluff wall, he heard a rustling noise followed by the sound of stones tumbling down the bluff. Someone was nearby!

Hunkering down in the shadows of some twisted spruce trees, he waited breathlessly. Was it possible the cop was really that fast? The rustling sound grew closer, but because of the wind, he couldn't determine which direction it was coming from. Fearing the worst, Jon tried to think of a plan. Should he try to sneak up on him? Jump him from behind? Try to get his gun? And then, if he did, what was next? He'd have to figure some way to safely detain the creep and find a place to call for help. But even then, who would he call? What if his mom was right? What if some of the local police were as crooked as this guy? What if they were all in cahoots? Whatever he did, Jon couldn't let the "cop" take control of the situation. If he did, he'd be dead, for certain.

Just as he was bracing himself for more hand-to-hand combat, he heard a whimpering noise. It sounded like an animal. Cupping his hand to his ear, he listened intently. *Ralph?* Jon slowly stood and, peering over the tall beach grass, saw a long blonde ponytail blowing in the breeze. It was the runner!

Not wanting to startle her, he controlled himself from rushing at her. Instead, he slowly approached, waving his arms in silence. And when she recognized him, he hurried over.

"You're okay," she whispered, relief washing over her face as they crouched down in the tall grass together.

A shock tore through him as he noticed her pale blue

shirt soaked with blood. "Were you shot, too?" he quietly demanded.

"No, no, I'm okay," she said in a hushed tone. "That's from Ralph." She pointed to where Ralph was relieving himself in the tall grass. "Just a flesh wound. He'll be okay." She glanced down at Jon's makeshift bandage. "What about you?"

"A flesh wound, too," he quietly assured her. "I can run fairly well."

"You and Ralph are fortunate," she said.

"Yeah. *Officer* Krantz is a bad shot."

"Officer *Krantz*?" she whispered.

"I noticed the name on his badge when we were scuffling."

"There's no way he's a real cop."

"I'm sure you're right. Or if he is, he's a crooked one." He glanced over his shoulder. "We better get moving. My guess is he's following. I'd hoped you'd gone the other way."

"I planned to turn back in a while. I was headed for the creek, hoping to hide my footprints." She pointed to the fog bank. "Then I was going to cut across the beach and double back in the surf."

Jon stared at her in wonder. "Yeah, that's exactly what I was going to do, too."

"But I thought the creek was closer." She frowned.

"It's still about a mile down the beach." He stooped over to pick up Ralph. "We better get—" He stopped to the sound of rustling grass—and there was no wind blowing. "Go," he whispered to her. "Fast."

Before he could stop her, she grabbed Ralph from

his arms. And then she took off and he followed. They hadn't gone twenty feet before he heard the sound of a gunshot—and unless he was wrong, the source was from a high-powered rifle this time—not a revolver. "Stay low," he called out as he followed her.

Despite the pain in his leg, he knew he had to run with every ounce of his strength. Not that he could keep pace with her. And for that he was glad. If Krantz was going to catch one of them, he wanted it to be him. To his surprise, the woman was heading inland now, going right into the rolling dunes, which would put them out in the open for a few dangerous seconds. But realizing her strategy—hoping to outrun Krantz through the uneven ups and downs of the sand dunes—he followed. Two more shots rang out just as she made it into the cover of the grassy area and one more before he dived into the grass, rolling down the hill toward her. Even though they were leaving a trail by running through the valley in this dune, he knew this was their best hope. To wear Krantz out and to convince him that they were heading for the jetty. If only Jon didn't expire first.

After about fifteen minutes of running up and down dune hills, the woman stopped to wait for him. He could barely breathe, let alone talk, but he pointed toward the ocean.

"The creek?" she asked breathlessly.

He nodded. And now they jogged through another section of dune grass, working their way toward the bluff. Jon's mind was racing now. Who was this Krantz guy anyway? He had to be involved in something really sinister.

Jon's chest felt as if it were about to burst as they reached the bluff. To his dismay the fog bank hadn't made it all the way across the beach yet.

"Do you think we lost him?" the woman asked between breaths.

"Don't know," he gasped.

"Should we go for it?" She pointed toward the creek that cut across the beach.

He just nodded. And together they scrambled and slid down the sandstone face of the bluff. When they reached the beach level, he motioned to her to wait, pressing his back against the concave rock wall. Just in case Krantz was up above. Straining his ears, he listened, but all he could hear was the sound of his own heavy breathing and the waves. He looked out to where the fog bank was slowly crawling across the sand.

"Should we wait for the fog?" she whispered.

He looked at the bluff overhead, imagining a winded Krantz posted up there with his powerful rifle. They would be easy pickings, making their way through the creek. Jon patted a damp driftwood log that the tide had pushed up against the bluff wall. "Let's wait."

"Let me fix that," she said quietly, pointing to the bandage he'd made from a shirt. "I'm nearly done with nursing school." She handed Ralph to him. "Might as well put it to use." She knelt down and went to work.

"Thanks." He used his hand to wipe the sweat from his brow. He couldn't remember ever feeling this tired before.

"You're right," she whispered. "It's not a deep wound." She bound it up more tightly, tying the sleeves of his shirt into a more secure knot and tucking the loose pieces into his makeshift bandage. "Hopefully that'll hold awhile."

Jon held a finger to his lips, nodding to where he thought he'd heard a noise above them. Just then some small stones tumbled down. He slipped his hand around Ralph's snout to muzzle him, holding him close to his chest. The sound of barking could prove lethal for all of them right now.

The girl looked down at Ralph and, as if sensing the dog's fear at being muzzled like this, she gently stroked his head and scratched his ears. Jon could feel the small animal slowly relaxing. And still up against the wall and not moving, they remained silently frozen in place for about ten or fifteen minutes. Long enough to catch their breath, and hopefully long enough for Krantz to move on.

Jon nodded to where the fog was nearly to the bluff. He pointed at the woman now, silently indicating that she should remain put while he ventured out. His thinking was that, if he was visible from the bluff above, he'd make an easy potshot—for someone with good aim, that is. But if the cop was going to take him out, Jon wanted the woman to still have a chance. So, holding the muzzled dog, he headed out in the stream, hoping and praying that the fog was thick enough to conceal him—and at the same time bracing himself for the sound of shots and the impact of bullets…and death. But at least she would be safe…or so he hoped. Why hadn't he gotten her name?

Finally, just as it grew hard to see her, he waved with one hand, motioning for her to join him—and hoping she would hurry. To his relief, she sprinted through the creek, and now they ran full speed toward the ocean, where their footsteps would be washed away forever. Turning north, they continued running through the surf. But it would be at least an hour before they reached safety—if that were even possible. And that was only if they ran at full speed—which Jon wasn't sure he could do.

"You're faster," Jon said breathlessly. "Take the lead."

"No," she firmly told him. "I want to stay with you. Your leg's wounded." She held out her hands. "Let me carry Ralph—it's the least I can do."

He reluctantly relinquished the dog, trying to run faster, but soon realized it took all his energy just to maintain a fast jog. "What's your name?" he huffed as he struggled to keep pace with her, water splashing with each step.

"Leah," she told him. "Leah Hampton."

"I'm Jon." He gasped for air. "Jon Wilson."

"Nice to meet you, Jon." She smiled, and for a moment he felt the sun had burst through the fog, and his steps grew lighter.

"In a while," he huffed, "we'll run—beside the water. The tide—coming in—hide our footprints."

"Good idea." She nodded. "We'll make better time that way."

"Yeah."

"Where are we going?"

"Home," he puffed. "I hope."

So many questions were tumbling through his head, but it was impossible to ask them. Who was she? Where did she live? Why had she been stopped? It took all his energy just to keep moving—and moving quickly. His only hope was that they would outrun and outwit Krantz. But even if they made it back to his parents' beach house without being caught or shot, they would still be cut off from most of the world. There was no landline there, and Jon's cell phone was useless in these parts.

Not only that, but his Fiat was in the garage with its carburetor removed and totally dismantled. It had seemed a good idea yesterday. So, other than his parents' three-wheeled bikes and his dad's less than dependable quad runner, they would have no transportation. And the nearest vacation cabins—as far as Jon had observed this past week—were all empty right now. The closest "civilization" was a little mom-and-pop store four miles away that kept random hours in the off-season. And then it was another eight miles to town.

When Jon had asked to borrow his parents' beach cabin as a "getaway" he hadn't planned on getting away quite like this. He peered through the fog toward the dark shadow of the bluff that ran alongside the beach. In places where the fog was patchy, he could see clear to the top of it. Could Krantz see them, too?

"We gotta move faster," he huffed at Leah, as if she were the one slowing them down, when he knew she could've been a mile ahead by now.

"Here." She held Ralph close to her with one arm, hooking the other arm into his, and then, keeping stride—pace for pace—she gradually increased the speed, pushing him harder and harder. If the crazy cop didn't shoot him, he'd probably drop dead from a heart attack right here on the beach before long. But at least he'd have a beautiful woman by his side.

THREE

Leah knew she was pushing Jon too hard, but the image of that cop's enraged face and the way he'd pulled out his gun seemed to be driving her. It was obvious that if "Officer" Krantz found them again, he would shoot first and ask questions later...if they were even alive later. As it was, she suspected Krantz wanted them both dead. *But why?*

She glanced at Jon, knowing that he was exhausted and in pain. He probably couldn't last much longer, but she knew they had to keep moving—had to find safety. Jon had said "home," but she wasn't even sure what that meant. Did he live along this beach somewhere? She thought most, if not all, of the homes along here were vacation cabins. In fact, she'd been warned by several people that this desolate part of the beach wasn't a safe place for a lone runner during the "off-season." Too bad she hadn't listened.

Jon's pace slowed and then he stopped completely. Bending over and clasping his sides, he panted loudly, trying to catch his breath.

"Are you okay?" she asked breathlessly. "Was the pace too much?"

"No," he gasped. "Need speed."

"I know." She peered through the fog, spotting some thin places where they could be seen and shot at. The sun was going down but not quickly enough to hide them in the darkness.

Still hunched over, Jon nodded toward shore. "Turn here."

"Let's go." She linked his arm again, tugging him into the creek.

Jon stumbled a couple of times, but she managed to keep him on his feet. And it wasn't long before they were across the stretch of beach. From there Jon led them alongside the bluff until he finally stopped at what appeared to be some steep stone steps, carved right into the bluff. "This way," he puffed.

Still cradling Ralph in her arms, she let Jon lead the way up the steps, giving him nudges with her shoulder when his footsteps slowed. She knew he was struggling. He'd lost blood and was dehydrated. Even though the gunshot wound didn't look too serious, it had to be hurting. And if it didn't get cleaned out, infection could set in.

Through the fog, a large dark shape emerged before them on top of the bluff. It appeared to be a house and as they got closer, she saw that it was made of dark gray stone, similar to the rocky cliff it sat upon. Relief washed through her as Jon led them through an overgrown hedge and across a mossy patio to a back door. He dug in the pocket of his cargo shorts, producing a key. Before long, he'd unlocked the door and led her inside to an enclosed porch that was also a laundry room. "Must lock up," he said between breaths. "No lights."

Still panting, Jon locked the porch door, then quickly punched some numbers into a keypad that must've been linked to a security system. That was somewhat reassuring. He led them into what appeared to be a kitchen, locking that door, as well. Only illuminated by the last rays of dimming gray light, the old-fashioned room looked slightly eerie—almost like a scene from an old horror movie. Leah suddenly wondered what she was doing here—with a perfect stranger—or if she was even safe. After all, she didn't even know this man. Not really. Still, it was better than being out there with the crazy cop imposter.

Leah's mind attempted to replay the mad race up and down the beach, the gunshots, being stopped by the cop. It all felt surreal now. The fact that a "cop" wanted them dead was mind-boggling. In fact, none of this made any sense. How had she gotten herself into such a mess? But somehow, holding the warm little dog in her arms and seeing Jon's stressed but handsome face peering curiously at her brought a sense of reassurance to her.

"Are you okay?" he asked.

"I kind of feel like I'm in shock."

"Me, too." Jon was still breathing heavily as he reached for Ralph. "Thanks. For helping with him."

"We need to hydrate," she told him.

He retrieved a couple of water bottles from a case sitting on the counter, handing her one. As she opened it, Jon filled a bowl with water, setting it on the floor for Ralph to lap. Then he took a long swig from the water bottle.

"You should probably have something besides just straight water to hydrate." She glanced around the small kitchen. Her eyes had adjusted to the lack of light and she could take in the surroundings. Old-fashioned cabinets, a small kitchen table, a gas stove with pots hanging above it. "Your electrolytes are probably low. Do you have some juice or soda or something?"

"Here." Jon handed her a beach towel. "Hold that up while I open the fridge—to block the light from showing—just in case anyone's around to see it." She held up her "screen" as he opened the fridge. He quickly snagged a bottle of orange juice and a couple of sodas, then closed the door. "There." He handed her a can of soda.

"We need to cleanse your wound," she said after she nearly drained her water bottle. "And Ralph's, too. Do you have any first-aid supplies here? And is there a place where we can turn on more lights so that I can examine the wounds?"

Jon pointed at the window above the sink. "Light will leak through those shutters." He carried Ralph toward a dark hallway. "But we can black out the bathroom window. And there's a first-aid kit in there."

As Leah followed him, she noticed lights flashing in another part of the house. "Jon," she whispered urgently, tugging on his shirt. "Look!"

As he turned around, she motioned for him to bend down low, pointing to a window in the front of the house where the light had flashed through. "It looked like some sort of searchlight," she whispered.

"Here." He slipped Ralph into her arms. "Keep him quiet. And go down the hallway. First door to your right is the basement. Go lock the door, and muzzle him while I investigate."

Staying low, Jon crept into the front room in time to spot a police cruiser slowly driving by, flashing a searchlight all around the yard and finally moving on to do the same to the next cabin. This wasn't the unmarked car that Krantz had been driving, but a well-marked cruiser that was obviously looking for someone. Not good news, since it seemed to suggest that Krantz might really have police connections after all.

Jon watched as the cruiser slowly made its way to the next cabin, once again sweeping it with a bright beam of light, shining it up and down and all around with dogged determination. How long would it take them to figure out that he and Leah were holed up here? And what then?

Staying low, Jon made his way to the basement door, quietly tapping on it, whispering that it was him and waiting to hear the lock clicking. The door opened and, even in the semidarkness, Jon could sense her fear.

"Is he gone?"

Jon just nodded. He wasn't sure he wanted to tell her about the police cruiser just yet. That would probably just scare her even more. It had certainly shaken him to think that Krantz wasn't working alone.

"What should we do?" she asked.

"We need a plan."

"And we need to tend those wounds," she told him.

He led her to the bathroom, where he hung several towels over the flimsy curtain that covered the small window. But, still not convinced the towels would keep out the light, he got a roll of duct tape, then securely taped all the possible cracks, finally turning on the light above the sink. They both blinked at the brightness of the room, and Ralph actually wagged his tail. Jon grabbed another towel, shoving it against the crack at the bottom of the door. Just in case.

"Poor little guy." Leah set Ralph in the claw-foot tub. "We need to clean you up." She turned to Jon. "But I suggest we do you first." She frowned as she started to scrub out the sink. "I wish we could boil some water."

"Really?" He frowned. "I thought that was just in movies."

"Do you have rubbing alcohol?"

"My mom probably does. Dad teases her that she should've been a doctor instead of a lawyer." He opened the large linen closet where his mom stocked all sorts of medical things, including a first-aid kit that he handed to her. Then he started reading the labels from various bottles. "Cough suppressant, aspirin, hydrogen peroxide, milk of magnesia, Neosporin, witch hazel, iodine, rubbing alcohol—"

"Impressive." She reached for the rubbing alcohol, using it to douse the already cleaned sink, then, plugging the drain, she filled it with warm water, then added a little more rubbing alcohol. "To purify the water," she explained as she removed some clean washcloths from a nearby shelf. "Why don't you take a seat on the edge of the tub? Less messy that way."

Jon petted Ralph as he sat on the edge of the tub, trying not to wince as Leah meticulously cleansed the wound and surrounding area. She applied some iodine around the wound, then Neosporin on the wound.

"It looks pretty clean," she told him. "From what I can see, it's not deep enough to harm muscle." As she pushed a piece of gauze onto the opening, Jon took in a sharp breath. "Sorry," she said as she pushed another layer of gauze over the first one, securing them with adhesive medical tape. "You could probably use some stitches, but this should hold you for a while." She looked up at him with a puzzled expression. "I mean, I don't even know what we're going to do from here. But this should keep infection at bay." She stood up straight, reaching for the bottle of disinfecting hand soap again. "And now it's your turn, Ralph."

Jon swung his legs around, drying them on a towel, then moving out of the way. He watched with interest as she tended to Ralph, talking gently to him the whole time as she washed the blood off his coat, then finally cleansed and bandaged his wound.

"You're really good at this." Jon handed her a clean towel, waiting as she wrapped it around Ralph, gently absorbing the water. "I know my mom will be appreciative that you rescued her dog. Thanks, Leah."

"I'm the one who should be thanking you." She stood up straight as Ralph gave a shake to his coat. "If you and Ralph hadn't shown up when you did—" She visibly shuddered. "Well, I can't even imagine where I'd be right now. But I'm sure it wouldn't be good." Fear washed over her features again. "What if he comes back, Jon? What will we do?"

"Just what we're doing now? Act like nobody's home. There's no reason he should suspect we're in this particular house. I've been a hermit since I got here. And I haven't seen a single neighbor around. No one knows that I'm here."

"So you think he's just checking all the houses along here?"

"That's my guess."

She pointed at Ralph. "But what if he comes back? What if he knocks on the door, and Ralph barks and gives us away?"

"He doesn't normally do that. In fact, that whole thing with Krantz was totally out of character for old Ralph."

"But he's been through a lot," she said. "Maybe he's not being his normal self."

"Good point. Being in pain might be a factor." Jon went to the linen closet again. "My mom sometimes gives Ralph tranquilizers during long car trips. The vet prescribed them to help with Ralph's anxiety. I gave him one for our trip down here from Portland. Worked like a charm." He found the bottle and held it up. "Voilà."

"And good rest helps patients to heal."

He slipped the bottle of pills into his pocket. "I'll need to put it into some canned dog food to get it down." Jon frowned as he remembered the police cruiser. "There's something I need to tell you." Realizing she was shivering, he decided to wait. "But first you need some dry, warm clothes to wear. We both do."

She looked down at her running clothes, then glumly nodded.

"You're probably about the same size as my mom." He studied her slender figure as she wrapped the towel around Ralph again, picking him up. "Well, thinner, but I'll go grab something for you."

"Better turn off the light before you open the door," she warned as she sat on the toilet seat lid, cradling Ralph in her lap like an infant. "Just in case."

"Yeah." He clicked off the light, then slipped out into the darkness, feeling his way down the hallway to his parents' room, where despite the drapes he was still reluctant to turn on a light. He fumbled his way over to the closet, wishing he'd thought to grab a flashlight. But, feeling around, he finally located what felt like a set of warm-ups hanging on a hook on the back of the door. His mom's favorite beach garb—sweatpants and a hoodie sweatshirt. Even if they were a little too big for Leah, they would be clean and warm.

Leah talked quietly to Ralph as they sat in the pitch-black darkness together. "It's okay, boy," she said gently. "You're going to be okay now." She knew her words were as much for her as for him, but it was reassuring to feel him starting to relax a little.

But she jumped as the bathroom door opened. "I found something for you," Jon said as he closed the door, then turned on the light. He held up a velour jogging suit.

"Purple," she said with raised brows. "Interesting."

He frowned. "Sorry. It was dark in there. I couldn't see the color."

"I'm not complaining." She smiled. "I've just never been a fan of purple." She reached to touch the soft fabric. "But it does look warm. Thanks!"

"I'll get this guy some food." Jon took Ralph from her. "Go ahead and clean up and change. Just douse the light before you come out because I, uh, I noticed the police car still cruising around out there."

"You mean Krantz's unmarked car?" she asked with concern.

Jon's brow creased. "No, it's a marked car."

"A marked car? A *real* police car?"

"Yeah. From the city. According to my parents, they don't usually patrol out here much. I mean, we're out of the city limits. But the county doesn't patrol these parts at all. So I guess they've sort of contracted it to the city. But my dad always says it's kind of a no-man's-land out here."

Half of what he said went over her, but the one fact she could hold on to was that a police cruiser was patrolling around, probably looking for them, and it wasn't Krantz. "What does this mean?" she whispered.

"I'm not sure." He pointed to the purple warm-ups. "You're cold. Get those on and I'll go feed Ralph some food and a tranquilizer. And then we can talk." He sighed. "And attempt to figure this mess out."

"It is a mess, isn't it?"

He just nodded, turning off the light, then opening the door and leaving, closing the door behind him.

Ten minutes later Leah emerged from the bathroom considerably warmer and dryer in Jon's mother's sweatpants and hoodie, having freshened up a bit in the sink, rinsed her soiled running clothes and hung them in the bathtub to dry. A real bath sounded lovely. But not here. Not now. Not with Krantz and his "pals" prowling the neighborhood. What was going on anyway?

As she tiptoed through the unlit and quiet kitchen, she noticed lights outside and suddenly, like before, the bright beam was passing through the house's interior again. Afraid her silhouette might show up, she hit the floor, waiting behind the kitchen doorway as the startling searchlight swept over the premises. Had they figured it out?

When the light beam was pointing away from her, she crawled past the entry to the kitchen. Her heart pounded in fear as she wondered where Jon and Ralph were hiding. Surely they hadn't left the house. Jon wouldn't abandon her here by herself. Then, remembering the few minutes she had crouched in pitch-black darkness behind the locked door on the basement stairs, she decided to try it again.

She was just crawling toward the hallway when she heard a loud pounding on the front door. Bracing herself for the sound of Ralph's barks, she prayed that he'd stay quiet. The pounding persisted, almost as if someone felt certain this was their hideout. "Open up!" a voice yelled as another ray of light swept through the windows in front—flashing over the shadowy furnishings in a way that made her feel like a hunted animal. Like someone's prey. She remained frozen, cowering by a china hutch, and still a few feet from the hallway and the door to the basement. Praying for invisibility, she felt her heart lurch with each loud bang on the door.

"I know you're in there!" a loud male voice boomed through the wooden door. Probably Krantz's. "Come out, or I'm coming in!"

Seeing the light sweeping the other side of the house, Leah made her break through the darkness, quietly scrambling to the safety of the hallway, where she crouched against the wall and waited in fear while Krantz continued pounding and shouting. Certain he was about to kick down the front door, she tried to think—what could she do?

She reached up to try the doorknob to the basement, but it was locked. She suspected Jon and Ralph had gone down there and considered knocking on it, but was afraid it might get Krantz's attention. And what if Jon opened it with a light on down there? As Krantz continued to pound and shout, she wondered if he really did have a search warrant—and if so, could he legally kick down the door? But then she decided that was just as bogus as him having an arrest warrant for her. But why had he made such a claim? What had been his real intent? And why was he so relentless in his search for them? Well, aside from the fact that they could both accuse him of attempted murder. That was probably more than enough to make him want to silence them.

Just when it felt as if her heart were about to hammer out of her chest, the basement door cracked open and she heard Jon whispering, "Come on. *Hurry.*"

"Wait," she whispered back, watching as the flashlight swept through the front room again. Even though it didn't reach into the hallway, she was too scared to move. Then, as it illuminated the other side, she slipped around the opened door, entered the basement and silently closed and locked the door behind her, then sat on the steps, trying to hold back tears of fear and desperation.

"You're trembling," Jon said in a low murmur as he put an arm around her shoulders. "I'm guessing it's not from being cold."

"Krantz is out there," she reported in a hushed tone. "He's beating on the door—right now. Can't you hear it?"

"I thought I heard something, but I hoped it was you."

"Listen," she whispered frantically. "That's him pounding—he's threatening to kick the door down."

Jon pulled her closer, holding her a little tighter. "There's nothing we can do about that right now."

"But what if he does break in?" she asked in a shaky voice. "What if he kicks the door in and enters the house?"

"Then we'll get him charged with breaking and entering as well as attempted kidnapping, attempted murder, reckless endangerment and several other substantial charges that should get him locked up for a while." Jon's voice didn't sound nearly as brave as his words insinuated. Not that she could blame him. She was so scared she felt sick to her stomach. "We've got so much on him that, once he's convicted, he'll be put away for a long time, Leah."

"Not if he kills us first—that's what he wants to do.

I know it." She let out a little sob. "What is wrong with him? Why is he doing this? Why won't he just leave us alone?"

"Because we know too much about him."

"What do we really know?"

"Just that he's hiding behind his badge while breaking the law. That he's a bad cop. That's enough to make him worried. And my suspicion is that we've only scratched the surface with him. This guy has a lot to hide. Enough to make it worth his while to get rid of both of us."

She didn't doubt that. Even so, it brought no comfort. No hope. As they sat there clinging to each other on the inky staircase, she knew that her only hope—their only hope—was God. She prayed for God's help—and for the faith to believe He really could deliver them from this madness.

FOUR

When the banging overhead finally ceased, Jon kept his arm around Leah, both of them just sitting there and listening to the silence. Finally he helped her to stand and gently guided her down the steep dark stairs.

"Careful," he warned quietly.

"Do you think he's really gone? That he gave up?"

"It sounds like it."

"But why was he so insistent?" she continued. "Do you think he really *knows* we're in here?"

"I honestly don't see how."

"Maybe we left footprints outside," she suggested. "Our feet were wet and sandy."

"But the back patio is already wet and sandy. Plus it's mossy," he said. "I can't imagine any footprints would show up."

Leah wanted to believe him, but the sound of Krantz yelling kept echoing through her head. At the foot of the stairs, Leah thought she could see a very faint light in the room. As they moved closer, it seemed to be flickering like a flame. Was Krantz going to burn them out? "What's that?" she asked in alarm. "That light? Where's it—"

"It's okay," Jon said soothingly. "Just a candle. Not visible outside. There are no windows down here." He led her around a corner where she was surprised to see a small yellow candle bravely burning in a glass jar in the center of a wooden crate that appeared to be serving as a makeshift coffee table in front of a shabby-looking couch and a couple of wicker chairs.

"The light's nice," she said quietly. "I couldn't even see it from the stairs."

"Good."

By the candle's flickering flame, she could see by the trails of dust that things had been moved around. Probably to make it more comfortable—as if they might be down here awhile. But what if Krantz broke in—and started shooting? Perhaps they should barricade the door, too.

"Have a seat," Jon said gently.

She sat down in a wicker rocker, hugging her arms around her middle and trying to shake off the terror still seeping through her. "I don't understand why Krantz is so driven. He really sounded as if he plans to break in here—as if he wants to kill us."

"Well, if he does, the alarm will go off."

"The alarm?" she asked hopefully.

"Yeah. My parents' security system. But it might not help much…since it's the police department in town that will be notified. And Krantz might end up fielding that call for them."

"And he'd tell them it was a false alarm," she surmised.

"Probably." Jon reached for a metal baseball bat leaning against a cardboard box. He swung it up, smacking it into his open palm as if it were a weapon—and not just a youth's toy. He pointed the bat to a small "arsenal" of other random pieces. A plumbing wrench, a long metal pole, several large kitchen knives, some lengths of rope and a roll of wire, along with several other slightly threatening-looking pieces. He must've collected them while she was cleaning up. But, really, she couldn't see how they'd be much use against Krantz.

"In case we need to defend ourselves," he said apologetically as he set the bat down. "Hopefully we won't."

"Hopefully." She shuddered to imagine using those "weapons" to ward off real firearms or even a SWAT team. Even if Krantz was a lousy shot, he could hit them eventually. Or one of his buddies would.

"I can't think of any reason Krantz would focus only on this house," Jon said. "My guess is he's just hitting up every house along this road. He's probably pounding on every door, just hoping to see or hear something that reveals our whereabouts. He's probably hoping he'll get Ralph to bark—to give us away."

"Speaking of Ralph, where is he?" she said suddenly. "Why wasn't he barking?"

"I put a tranquilizer in his food while you were cleaning up. He chowed down and passed out within minutes." He pointed to a crate where Ralph was nestled in an old army blanket. "Poor guy was exhausted. He probably didn't even need the pill, but we won't take any chances. And I've got another one already mixed into some dog food just in case he wakes."

"Good." Leah let out a long sigh, willing herself to relax. "This all feels so crazy and unreal—like we just got pulled into some weird crime TV show."

"I know. I keep trying to figure it all out. Kind of makes my head hurt. And more than figuring it out, I want to figure a *way* out. I'm just not sure what it is." He explained how he'd been working on his car the past couple of days. "So it's not running at the moment." He shared the other various plans that he'd been concocting, but they all had fatal flaws.

"But can't we fix your car?" she asked. "I mean, we'd have to wait until the cop cars stop patrolling in order to drive safely out of here, but—"

"My carburetor is in about a hundred pieces," he said glumly. "It was having problems on the trip down here. I thought I'd be clever and fix it myself." He explained how he and his dad had torn apart and reassembled numerous cars over the years. "It didn't seem like a big deal…at the time. And it's not, except that it'll take hours to put it all back together."

"How long?" she asked eagerly. "What if we go work on it now? Maybe I can help."

"We'd need to cover all the windows in the garage to keep light from going out—that alone might look suspicious. And even if it went smoothly, it could take all night. Even then, I'm not sure it would work. Some of the pieces looked pretty worn. I was going to call in to town to see if I could get some parts delivered out here."

"Your phone," she said. *"It works here?"*

"Not in the house. I have to go climb up onto this rock—it's about a quarter mile down the road—just to get one bar, and even that's dicey if the weather is bad."

"Oh." She pursed her lips. "But we could do that, couldn't we? We could go try your phone… I mean, if the cop cars aren't parked out there."

"Yes." He nodded slowly. "We could. And I'm thinking we should call the state police first. But only when we know it's safe to get to the rock. It's kind of exposed to the road." He pointed to some food on the makeshift table with the candle. "Maybe we should eat something first. Just to fortify ourselves…you know, for whatever lies ahead." He handed her a box of rye crackers as he cut some slices of cheese. "Sorry there's not much to choose from. I just grabbed what was handy."

"And you're certain no one knows you're here in this house?" she asked as she helped herself to an apple and bit into it. "No neighbors or anyone who could help?"

"Pretty certain. Ralph and I got here on Saturday—the same day we spotted you running on the beach." He shook his head. "Here I was kicking myself for not getting your name…and now here you are stuck with me."

She made a weak smile. "I don't mind being stuck with you." She just wished the circumstances were different. "So no one saw you coming or going here?"

"I got groceries on my way here," he explained. "Then I parked my car in the garage. And other than walking on the beach—and I always use the back door for that—I haven't left the house."

"You say this is your parents' house—do they know

you're here? Any chance they could help somehow?" She reached for a piece of cheese.

"They're on a two-week cruise to celebrate their fortieth anniversary."

"Sounds nice." She sighed.

"How about you?" he asked. "Will anyone notice you're missing?"

She shrugged. "Probably not… Not for a while anyway."

"Did anyone know where you went to run?"

"I mentioned I was going running to a friend at work. But I didn't say where." She frowned. "Stupid… I know."

"And there's no one who'd go out looking for you? No husband or boyfriend? No roommate?"

She peered curiously at him. It almost felt as if he were fishing. "No," she said firmly. "No husband. No boyfriend. My life's been pretty busy the past couple of years. No time for that sort of thing."

"Right."

"But I do live with my great-aunt."

"So she'll know you're missing?" he asked hopefully.

"Probably not. She's elderly and I live in an apartment over her garage. We can go days without seeing each other."

"Oh." He frowned.

"How about you? Anyone who will wonder where you are? Any significant other?"

"I could probably be missing for a week and no one would notice."

"That sounds rather sad."

"Well, it's because I took some time off work. You see, I was house- and dog-sitting for my parents in Portland and it seemed like a good opportunity to have a break. So I brought Ralph to the beach. I planned to stay for a week or two."

"That must be nice."

"What?"

"To be able to take a week or two off from work… to come to the beach whenever you like." It sounded like a different world to Leah. One that she couldn't help but envy.

He shrugged. "The truth is, I was thinking about quitting my job. I told my boss I needed time to think about it."

"Didn't you say you were an attorney? Or was that just to make Krantz worried?"

"I am an attorney. But I work in a firm that mostly practices corporate law. Not really what I'd planned to do with my life."

"So what did you plan to do with your life?" She took a drink of water.

"I wanted to be an artist."

She blinked as she set down the water bottle. "Seriously?"

"Yeah. That's pretty much everyone's reaction." He frowned. "But I've always been into art. Drawing and painting and even some sculpting. My parents talked me into getting my law degree. They're both attorneys. They figured if I finished law school, I'd have something to fall back on if my artistic abilities didn't pay off. But between law school and working, I haven't been able to pursue art at all. That's why I decided to take some time away. And it was easier to do with my parents out of the country."

"Until you got mixed up with me and Krantz."

"Speaking of Krantz, I think I'll slip up and see if he's cleared out. Maybe this is our chance to go use the phone."

"I'll come with you," she said quickly.

"Okay, but you wait in the hallway until I know the coast is clear."

She listened intently as she waited in the shadowy hall, but other than the gentle sound of the surf, she could hear nothing. Was it possible that Krantz had given up on them? She didn't think so.

"Come on," Jon called from the kitchen. "Let's make a break for it."

He led her out the back door, quietly locking everything behind them. And then he took her out to where the property overlooked the ocean. "We'll have to pick our way along the back side here," he explained, "going through the neighbors' yards. Too risky to be near the road."

It didn't take long before they reached the place where the bluff gave way to a rocky rise and Jon showed her the way to climb up to the top. "Stay low," he warned quietly as he shielded the light from his phone with his hand. "And keep an eye on the road. You see anyone, just nudge me and I'll stop talking. Okay?"

"Got it." Hunched down, she stared out toward the road, which, like everything else, was blanketed in fog. She could hear the sound of his phone and then he was asking for the number of the Oregon State Police—and being connected.

Leah listened to the conversation, hearing Jon telling the dispatcher where they were located and that they were in danger. Unfortunately the dispatcher was insistent upon sending out the local police.

"No," Jon said firmly but quietly—and for the second time. "*Don't do that.* We need the state police to—"

"The protocol is to inform the local police. They can get there sooner," she said stubbornly. "I'm going to contact them now."

"But we don't trust the local police," he argued. "Please, send out a state trooper and—"

"I am already connecting to your local dispatcher," she said. "If the local police need us for backup, we will be—"

"No, that won't—"

Leah elbowed him sharply as the lights from a car shone from around a corner. Even in the fog, she could see the reflective paint that implied it was a police cruiser. And not far behind it came what appeared to be the unmarked car. Probably manned by Krantz. She doubted that the cops could've heard them—unless their windows were open—but if a cop directed a spotlight up here, they would be easy to spot. "Get your face down," she hissed at Jon. And together they huddled against the rock, waiting for the cars to slowly move down the road.

"That dispatcher was worse than useless." Jon pocketed his phone.

"Who else can we call?" she whispered.

Just then a searchlight came washing over their rock, sending shivers of fear through Leah as she crouched low.

"Come on," Jon whispered, grabbing her hand. "We better beat it—fast."

Back on the bluff, he led her farther up and they worked their way past darkened vacation houses until they came to one clear at the end of the row. "I don't like damaging other people's property," Jon said as he picked up a large stone. With a crash he sent it through the front door's window. "But hopefully they'll understand, and I'll pay for repairs." He reached through the broken glass and opened the door, leaving it barely ajar. "Let's go," he said as he grabbed her hand, leading her down to the side of the bluff and onto the beach.

"Why did you do that?" she asked as they picked their way through a rocky area, clinging to the side of the bluff for cover.

"A smoke screen." Still holding her hand, he was leading her down the beach—heading south again.

"Oh, yeah. To throw them off."

"Might buy us some time. If they were distracted long enough, we might be able to make it past them and try walking to town."

"Do you think you could make it with your leg?" She noticed that he was limping.

"It hurts, but I think I can press through. The problem is that we'd have to take the main road. It'd be too rough to go cross-country. Not with the brush and swamps that run through here."

"Hey, what about my car?" she said suddenly. "Do you think it's still where I parked it? Maybe we could use it to get away." Of course, she knew this was pretty ridiculous. Her old Subaru couldn't outrun a police car if they were pursued.

"It's probably been towed." He paused to listen to something up above them, and she held her breath, waiting.

"If we got my dad's ATV running, we might make it to the jetty, then hike out on foot from there. But if we were spotted, they could easily pick us up on the other end."

"What should we do?"

"We need a good plan." He reached for her hand, leading her up the side of the bluff. "Let's go home and see if we can come up with something."

But before they could turn up the rock stairs that led to the house, they saw a pair of headlights on the beach, coming steadily toward them and sweeping a searchlight back and forth across the width of the beach as it approached.

"Come on." Grabbing her hand, Jon pulled her behind a driftwood log, throwing her to the ground as he flopped down beside her.

With wet sand in her face, Leah felt like sobbing— would this never end? And what if they'd been spotted just now? Her heart was pounding in her ears as she saw the light sweeping the beach, going back and forth like in a prison yard. And if they'd been seen, they'd be easy pickings down here on this desolate stretch of beach. No one would hear the gunshots. No one would call the police. And if their lifeless bodies were dragged out into the ocean, there would be no sign of them by tomorrow. They would be taken out with the tide. She shuddered as she desperately prayed for protection.

FIVE

After the car was a safe distance down the beach, Jon led Leah back up to the bluff and, seeing no cars or cops in sight, they snuck into the back of the house.

"I want to pull out a file my mom's been keeping," he told Leah after he locked the doors. "You go ahead and check on Ralph. If he's awake, urge him to eat some more. It might make him sleepy."

"What kind of file?" she asked as they stood in the dark hallway.

"I just remembered something my mom told me recently. She'd been saving articles related to what she believes might be a human-trafficking ring in the Northwest. Particularly around here."

"Human trafficking—seriously—in Cape Perpetua?"

"I know, it sounds a little far-fetched. Especially considering most people think Cape Perpetua is one of the safest beach towns on the Oregon Coast. My dad thinks my mom's being overly dramatic. But I'm beginning to wonder."

"Interesting."

"So I'll be digging around for a while. You stay down

there with the door locked. Don't open it unless you know it's me."

"Right." Her voice sounded small and shaky.

"We're going to be okay," he told her.

"How do you *know* that?" she asked in a doubtful tone.

"Because I believe it." He reached over to place a hand on her shoulder, suppressing the urge to pull her toward him in a comforting hug. "We can outsmart them, Leah. I know we can."

"Well, you must be a whole lot smarter than me." She made an attempt at a laugh, but it actually sounded pretty sad.

"Go check on Ralph," he told her. "And lock the door."

He waited to hear the sound of the lock clicking into place, then, staying low, he crept out to the kitchen to retrieve a flashlight from the junk drawer. He also pocketed some extra batteries and even got the small battery-powered radio that his mom kept tuned to a local station just in case of tsunami warnings, and set it by the door to the basement. Then, with the flashlight in hand, he crept into the small room next to his parents' bedroom. They used this space as their study. Although they both claimed that work was outlawed at the beach cabin, one or the other was usually caught going over a legal case from time to time. It was like a family joke and a natural consequence of two attorneys in one marriage.

One wall of the study was filled with a bookcase, and a large corner desk was situated by the window. The right side was used by his dad, and the left was his mom's. Both of them kept old-fashioned file cabinets—

a habit that Jon used to make fun of but something he was thankful for now as he used the flashlight to peruse through his mom's cabinet. It didn't take long before he found a manila file folder marked Human Trafficking in bold black ink. Tucking it under his arm, he was about to go down to the basement when he saw headlights moving down the road again. Would they never give up?

He crouched beneath the desk, remembering the glass window he'd smashed and hoping that he'd get the chance to make it up to the homeowners—that he'd live long enough to apologize and explain. But why hadn't that house kept the police busy for longer? Wouldn't they have searched it, turned it upside down? Or did it simply allow them to remove one possible cabin from their list of suspects? Perhaps he should've left more clues around, or chosen a larger house with more spaces to search through—although that would probably trigger a security alarm. But that might be a good thing if it sent additional cops out here. What was the chance that all the Cape Perpetua cops were crooked? They couldn't be—could they?

When the room became pitch-dark again, Jon quietly crept out and down the hallway. He was tempted to pull the drapes in the front room, but worried that might be a tip-off. Then he remembered the upstairs bedroom that he'd been using to paint in. Hadn't he pulled the shades down in there this afternoon when the sun got too hot? He tiptoed up the narrow staircase and was somewhat relieved to see that this room really was sealed off from the light. Not that they'd want to hide out up there, but it would be a change of pace from the dank basement.

Perhaps he could even offer Leah the twin bed to get some sleep tonight—while he kept watch downstairs to be sure she was safe. Before he left, he picked up his sketch pad and a packet of charcoal pencils. It wasn't as if he thought he was going to sketch anything while they were stuck in the basement trying to make an escape plan—but if things were different, if they were out of danger, he would love to do a sketch of Leah. She had the kind of face that lent itself to art. High forehead, straight nose, gorgeous cheekbones, ocean-colored eyes, full lips… He would like to paint her. If things were different. If they could somehow escape this thing alive.

As he tapped on the basement door, quietly identifying himself when he heard her on the stairs, he wondered what time it was. Although it felt as if it had been hours, maybe even days, since the shocking confrontation in the parking lot, he suspected it was probably not even nine o'clock yet. It would be a long night. He wondered how long it would take to rebuild that carburetor—or if it were even possible. But maybe it was worth a try.

"Here." He handed Leah the file folder, the radio and his sketch supplies when she opened the door. "I'm going to go get something. Lock the door." Before heading for the garage, Jon remembered how they'd left the bathroom. With its window covered in towels and signs of blood in the bathtub, it would be a dead giveaway in the event Krantz came into the house. So Jon went in and did a fast cleanup, trying to make it look normal, and finally removing the towels from the window and shoving them into the hamper.

He did a quick check of the kitchen, too, then, satisfied there were no traces of occupation, he crept out to the garage. With no signs of car lights outside, he knew this was his best chance to gather up the carburetor pieces and tools and take them down to the basement. If nothing else, a mechanical chore might keep his mind busy during the long night.

The garage felt more exposed than the rest of the house. Besides the windows in the garage door, the side door had a window in it and there was another window that faced toward the back. All were uncovered because his dad believed the sunlight was a good defense against the moisture and mildew so prevalent on the beach. But it made the garage feel a bit like a fishbowl. Jon tried to keep his flashlight hooded and pointed downward as he hurried to pile the carburetor pieces and necessary tools into a five-gallon bucket. He set a kerosene camp lantern on top.

He was just turning off the small flashlight when he heard the sound of a car engine—and once again, lights were moving around outside the house. Silhouettes of pine trees made sinister-looking shadowy images on the interior wall of the garage—moving back and forth with a persistence that sent a shiver of fear down his spine. Had someone seen signs of his flashlight just now? Jon reached for a nearby tire iron as he cowered against the garage door. As he waited for someone to come crashing through the side door, he thought he was ready to use it.

Crouching down with the tire iron in hand, he suddenly remembered his karate training as a kid—was it possible that he could put it to use now? Or was that just a young boy's delusion playing through his head? He remembered the Bruce Lee movies he watched with his dad. He was doubtful he could pull off those moves now. For the first time in his relatively peace-loving life, he wished he owned a gun. With his heart in his throat, he waited…and eventually the car moved on. But it had barely headed down the road when the second car came along—and it was followed by a third! Those guys were relentless. Three cars pursuing two innocent people. It was ridiculous. And disturbing. Was it possible that the entire Cape Perpetua Police Department was corrupt? Or had Krantz lied about what had happened? Were he and Leah considered fugitives?

Feeling more hopeless than ever, Jon crept back through the darkened house with his heavy bucket in hand. The wound in his leg was burning like fire, and every muscle in his body was starting to throb along with it. As badly as they needed to get out of here, he did not think he would be able to make it on foot. Besides, it would be too dangerous. For all he knew, there could be more than three cop cars cruising around right now. What if they brought in search dogs?

He tapped quietly on the basement door, hoping that Ralph was still asleep and not inclined to bark. Leah let him in and, not wanting to alarm her, he didn't mention that the searchers were still crawling all over the place—or that there were more. Instead, he told her his plan to work on the carburetor.

"If I can get it repaired and back into the car in the early hours of the morning, we might have a chance."

Although he knew he couldn't risk having lights on in there.

"Maybe the police shifts will be changing," she suggested hopefully. "Like around eight or so."

"Good thinking. So maybe we'll get a little break when they're not around. If the car is able to run, we'll just blast out of here and I'll drive at top speed all the way into town."

"Yes," she said eagerly. "If we make it to where people can see us, maybe go into a restaurant or grocery store—I think we'd be safe. The police wouldn't dare shoot at us in public, would they?"

"I don't think so." But even as he said this, he wasn't sure. Maybe the rest of the police thought they were dangerous criminals. Something about Krantz and the way those cars were persistently searching made him wonder what Krantz had told the force. Still, it seemed pointless to worry her any more than necessary.

He lit the kerosene lantern and laid out the carburetor pieces on top of a couple of cardboard boxes that he set up like a workbench. And as he started to clean the pieces and put them back together, he felt a false sense of security. Oh, he knew it was completely delusional, but as he listened to Ralph making quiet snuffling snores and the radio softly playing oldies, he felt himself relaxing. He glanced over to where Leah was reading something by candlelight…and for a blissful moment, he could almost imagine that nothing was wrong.

Except that this carburetor was looking even more shot than he'd imagined. Too many worn-out pieces—

and some that seemed to be gone. He needed a better plan.

"Listen to this!" Leah turned up the radio a bit.

"Local police are on the lookout for a pair of dangerous criminals tonight. Last seen in the north jetty beach area, a man and woman are suspected of being part of a drug-smuggling ring. During a routine stop, they assaulted and injured an officer, then got away on foot. The woman has been identified as twenty-four-year-old Leah Hampton. She is five foot eight, average weight, with blond hair and blue eyes, last seen wearing a blue tank top and black shorts. The unidentified man may be a transient. About six feet tall with shaggy brown hair and dressed in ragged clothing. Both are considered extremely dangerous. Anyone with information about this couple should contact the Cape Perpetua Police Department immediately. And the police warn citizens, do not engage with this couple. They are very dangerous."

Jon held up a wrench. "Yes, very dangerous. Right."

"Krantz is obviously trying to scare everyone away from us—in case we find someone we can ask for help."

"Plus it gives him a good excuse to shoot us if he wants."

"And I honestly think this has something do with it." She held up the folder. "In fact I'm sure it has everything to do with it."

"What have you found out?" He looked up from the mess of mechanical parts in frustration.

Leah picked up a piece of newsprint, waving it in the air. "I heard about this girl going missing last fall.

But everyone in town made it sound like she was a run-away—like she'd been having problems at home. But this is a piece that her mother wrote for the local paper. It's a plea for help—but it looks like they printed it in the letters-to-the-editor section and I'm guessing it got lost there. Kind of like the girl." Leah started to read from the clipping.

"I am Abigail Fowler's mother, and I am writing this letter to defend my daughter, who disappeared on November 19. In most ways Abigail is a typical teenage girl. She's had her ups and downs and occasionally disagrees with her parents. What sixteen-year-old doesn't? But Abigail was not unhappy at home! That report was completely false, and I want everyone to know it. Abigail is a good girl. And she was an honors student. She was applying at colleges all over the country. She is a quiet girl who kept to herself and didn't have a lot of friends. She had just finished cross-country and was looking forward to track season in the spring. Abigail had no reason to run away from home. None whatsoever. And no matter how many times I told the police this, they seemed to be convinced that I was lying. They assumed that because our marriage was having some problems, we were about to get a divorce and that she was distressed over this. That is a complete lie. Abigail had no reason to run away. I don't know why everyone wanted to believe that she did. I feel certain that my daughter was kidnapped. And if the police were doing their job they would be trying to find her instead of telling everyone that she's a troubled runaway. She is not! Please, help us find Abigail!

"Karen Fowler"

Jon laid down the wrench and went over to look at the file folder. "So I assume my mother thinks this Abigail girl is part of the human-trafficking problem? That she's been kidnapped by traffickers?"

"That seems to be the insinuation." She set the clipping down.

"What else did you find in there?"

"The other girl who went missing in early February actually did sound like she was a little on the wild side. Even her parents said as much. But there are parts of her story that suggest she didn't run away."

"Such as?" He sat down on the sagging sofa.

She picked up a photocopy of another article, scanning it. "Misha Campbell was only fifteen when she disappeared. Again, it's suggested that she's a runaway. And this time it's a little more believable. Except that this article mentions that Misha left her purse behind. It was found in a park near the beach. A place where Misha was reputed to have spent time with friends when they skipped school together. According to some of her friends, Misha was known for marijuana use."

"Well, if Misha was smoking and skipping school, it might be believable she could run away from home."

"Maybe, but to leave her purse behind? A purse that

not only had a little bit of money in it, but her cell phone, as well? I don't think so."

"Good point."

"What teen girl would willingly leave her cell phone behind?"

"Yeah…suspicious."

"Your mom thought it was suspicious, too."

"What else is in that file?" He picked it up, flipping through the papers.

"Just various articles from other newspapers in the Northwest. A few things she printed from the internet. And then there's this." She held up a dark-looking photograph that was printed on a piece of paper.

"What is it?" He peered at the smudgy photo. "Looks like a warehouse to me."

"See this." She pointed to handwriting at the bottom of the page. "'One-point-seven miles north of jetty.'"

"Huh?" He took the paper from her, studying it closely. "It looks like an ordinary warehouse."

"But look at that." She pointed to what appeared to be a portable outhouse off to one side.

"A porta-potty? So?"

"I don't know. It just seemed curious."

"Look at this." He pointed to a black shiny circle up high on a corner of the plain brown building. "That kind of looks like a fish-eye window—you know, the kind with a security camera in it, so that it can see around corners."

"Why would a warehouse need that? And what would a warehouse like that be doing 1.7 miles north of the jetty?" Leah asked. "There is nothing down there.

No houses, no industrial area, I don't think there's even a road in that section. Besides ATV use, and I'm not even sure about that, I think that part of the dunes is a protected area."

He scratched his head. "If there was a road down there, it would be pretty remote. We might be able to use it to get away."

"You mean you'll be able to drive your car?" She looked hopeful.

"Not likely." He shook his head. "For starters, I think the carburetor's shot. But if there is a road down on that end of the beach, I'm guessing we'd need to use my dad's ATV. Assuming that it runs, and that we could access the road from the beach. Those are a couple of big unknowns."

"I've run to the jetty and back a lot of times," Leah told him. "But I've never seen a road or any kind of development along there. It seems pretty desolate. Just brush and trees and dunes." She laid down the file folder. "In fact, I've often questioned the wisdom of running that lonely stretch by myself."

"For good reason." Jon frowned down at the photo. "This warehouse looks like it's surrounded by trees. I doubt it's even visible from the beach."

"I wonder how your mom found it."

"Well, she does like exploring. She takes wildflower walks, and collects mushrooms and picks huckleberries. She might've come across it accidentally."

"But the fact that it's *in this file*…" Leah picked up the folder. "Does she think it's related to these missing girls?"

"And her human-trafficking theory?" He frowned.

"Maybe it's not just a theory." Leah flipped through the papers in the file. "There's a lot of information here, Jon. Articles that seem to suggest that not only is human trafficking going on, but that it's rather common along the I-5 corridor—and along the Pacific Coastline."

"Wouldn't it be crazy if Krantz was involved in it?" Jon tried to make his words sound light, but his over-whelming feeling was that they were in way over their heads.

"I wish you could call your mom and ask her about the warehouse."

He rolled his eyes. "If we could call my mom, I'd ask her to send the FBI to come rescue us—ASAP."

"Yeah...duh." She made a weak smile. "Well, for what it's worth, I think your mom sounds interesting."

He nodded. "She is. You'd like her." He was thinking his mom would probably like Leah, too. Even though he could see she was pretty discouraged right now. "So tell me more about yourself, Leah. You're in nursing school, right?"

"At the community college. I'll graduate with my RN degree in June." She frowned. "I mean I hope I will. And I work at The Willows part time."

"The nursing home?"

"Yeah. And assisted living."

"Do you like working there?"

"It's kind of like killing two birds with one stone."

"How's that?" He studied her closely as she leaned back in the wicker rocker, a faraway look in her eyes. He wondered if he'd ever get the chance to paint her, imagining the highlights he'd use to give her hair that glow—like honey in the sunlight.

"My mom's a resident at The Willows."

"Oh? What's wrong?"

"She's got early-onset Alzheimer's," she said quietly. "She was in assisted care at first, but she was moved to the nursing home last fall."

"I'm sorry."

She nodded sadly. "Yeah. Me, too. But at least I get to see her when I go to work." She glanced at her watch. "Although it doesn't seem like I'll make it to my shift tomorrow. I'm supposed to be there by eight on Saturday mornings. But it's not like I can call in or anything…" Her voice trailed off.

"It's not morning yet." He considered slipping back outside, attempting to get some connectivity to call the FBI. But remembering the three cars he'd seen cruising the road while he was hunched down in the garage… and the discouraging dispatcher he'd reached during his last phone call attempt, he knew it wasn't worth the risk. Plus, his car was going to be useless, and they needed a better plan. A foolproof plan—if that were even possible.

"I want to be brave," she said softly, "but this feels so hopeless. Like we're trapped and will never—"

Just then a loud noise coming from upstairs made them both freeze. "Sounds like someone's breaking into the house," Jon whispered as he reached for the metal baseball bat, glancing over to where Ralph was still asleep.

Leah's blue eyes were wide with fear as Jon picked

up the chef's knife. He placed his forefinger over his lips and handed her the tire iron he'd brought down with him the last time. "I'll go by the door," he mouthed to her. "Stay here." He pointed to the candle. "Blow it out when I reach the top."

She just nodded.

Trying to be silent, he crept up the wooden stairs. Just as he positioned himself behind where the door would swing open—if it was soundly kicked—the candlelight from down below was extinguished. With the knife in his back pocket, he grasped the metal bat and waited. If the door came open, it would happen quickly. He just hoped he'd have the speed and presence of mind to whack the intruder over the head—before it was too late. Not that he wanted to kill anyone, even if it was Krantz. But he did want to stop him dead in his tracks.

Jon tilted his ear toward the door, listening to the sound of scuffling feet as well as the security alarm, which had gone off. This was followed by the sound of gruff male voices, signifying it wasn't just Krantz. Bracing himself for whatever was coming, Jon prayed a quick silent prayer—begging God to protect them— especially Leah. And, with his heart pounding in his ears, he waited.

SIX

Leah felt as if she were going to be sick to her stomach while she waited in the darkness, straining her ears to hear what was going on upstairs. All she could catch were the shrill tones of the home security system. Clutching the tire iron, she wondered if she should be prepared to defend herself. But against a gun? *How?* And for now, she knew her best defense was to follow Jon's direction and remain silent. All she could do was pray.

Ralph made a sleeping noise that made her jump, but she felt certain that it wouldn't be heard over the alarm still going on upstairs. After what seemed like hours, but according to her watch was more like thirty minutes, she heard the security alarm finally silenced. Still she was afraid to move and barely able to breathe evenly.

After another twenty minutes, she was relieved to hear the quiet squeak of Jon's footsteps on the wooden stairs. Surely he wouldn't come back down unless he knew they were gone. But why would they go without thoroughly searching the place? Or perhaps they didn't know about the basement? But wouldn't they have tried the door?

A flashlight suddenly illuminated the basement. She blinked at the brightness, squinting to see that Jon was approaching with a slightly relieved expression. Not for the first time, she thought how good-looking he was... how this could've been a lot more fun, under different circumstances.

"I think they're gone," he said. "At least from inside the house." He let out a tired sigh as he sank onto the sofa.

"Could you hear much?" She struck a match to light the candle.

"It sounded like three guys," he told her. "Cops, I'm sure. Krantz was there, too. But one of the cops was questioning Krantz. He demanded to know if Krantz had gotten a search warrant. Krantz claimed he had and then the other cop went out to his car to use his radio to call the alarm service. While he was gone, I could hear Krantz and his buddy scurrying around in a search of this house. He tried the basement door, too, but then kept on going to the other rooms. He was just trying our door again, but the cop who'd questioned him before came back in. He was furious at Krantz. Told him he was in hot water for not getting a search warrant and that he'd have to pay for the cost of the broken doors."

"So there's at least one honest cop?"

"Seems to be."

"I guess that's reassuring."

Jon nodded. "I almost considered going out to talk

to him, but I was afraid that Krantz would shoot me before I could open my mouth."

"He probably would've, too."

"Especially if he's involved in a human-trafficking scheme." Jon shook his head. "While I was up there by the door, I was thinking about that nasty business. What if Krantz really did kidnap those teen girls? What if he hid them in that warehouse my mom found? What if he planned to kidnap you, too?"

"I've been thinking the same thing."

"No wonder he wants us dead. We need a plan, Leah." Jon looked intently into her eyes.

"I know."

"I'd like to think we're safe down here. But knowing Krantz tried that door and knows it's locked, I wouldn't be surprised if he returns to check on it." Jon looked around. "In fact, let's move stuff around and make it look like no one's been down here."

"But where will we go?"

"Upstairs," Jon said as he started moving the furniture to make it look randomly stored. As he picked up Ralph's box, the dog woke up. "It's okay, boy," he said gently. "Just relocating." Before long, the basement looked like a storage room and they'd boxed their belongings and Ralph's things and were heading up the stairs. Jon led the way with his flashlight, quietly opening the door and listening before he pointed her down the hall and toward a narrow stairway.

"First door on your left," he whispered. "I'll bring the rest of the stuff and lock this door again."

Carrying a box of food and things, Leah tiptoed up

the stairs and, feeling her way to the door on the left, she went inside and waited. She hadn't felt particularly safe down in the basement, but at least it had a locking door. Now they were hiding in a room in a house where the doors had been broken open. Far from secure.

When Jon joined her, carrying Ralph's crate and some other things, she felt a tiny bit better, but still scared. He closed the door and turned on a flashlight, keeping the beam low.

"What about the window?" she asked with concern.

He produced a roll of duct tape. "I'll seal up the edges of this blind, but I think it's pretty solid."

While he taped off the window blind, she checked on Ralph. Although he was awake, she could tell his eyelids were heavy. Hopefully he'd continue resting peacefully.

"You can go ahead and light the candle," Jon told her as he slid a desk nearer to the door. "I want to go see if I can make a phone call from the rock—"

"I want to go with you," she said eagerly.

"I think it's safer for just one of us to go—less chance of being spotted."

"But what if they come back here?"

Jon frowned. "I can see the road from the rock. If I see them heading this way, I'll shoot right back." He pointed to the desk. "After I go, slide this in front of the door. If you hear anything below, just be quiet. I'm guessing Krantz wouldn't think to come back up here and waste time looking where he's already searched."

"I hope you're right."

Leah wanted to beg Jon to stay with her. What would she do if he were caught out there—if he were shot?

Wouldn't it be better for them to stay together? If she heard the sound of gunshots, she decided she would slip out of the house and then, even if it seemed impossible, she would begin a cross-country trek to town. She wasn't wounded like Jon was, and she was a strong runner. If she didn't wind up in a swamp with quicksand, she might eventually make it to town. Maybe by morning. Sure, it was a long shot, but it would be better than hiding out here like a sitting duck. She reached down to pet the groggy dog. But she'd have to leave him behind.

To distract herself from these fear-driven thoughts, Leah started looking around the room. Carrying the candle with her, she went over to look at some painting canvases that were stacked against the wall. The first one was of a seascape—a very beautiful scene with rocks and beach and ocean. It looked like a spot about twenty miles north of them. The next one was of two little girls and a dog on the beach. Also very nice.

She had already been convinced that Jon was a good artist—after she'd sneaked a peek at the sketchbook he'd left with her down in the basement. But seeing these paintings, she realized he was very talented. She came to the third and last painting—a portrait of a beautiful woman. Leah pulled it up to see better, holding the candle closer to illuminate the colors.

The young woman had a creamy complexion and wavy auburn hair that curled around her bare shoulders. But it was those emerald green eyes that captured Leah's attention. They were luminescent—and determined. There was no denying that this woman was gorgeous. She was also the same woman that had been a regular subject in Jon's sketchbook. Leah had seen numerous drawings of her and based on the female name scrawled across each one, Leah felt certain this "Monica" was someone who had been very important to Jon. She was also fairly sure that Jon was in love with her.

A noise downstairs made her catch her breath and, quickly laying down the canvas, she blew out the candle and listened to the sound of footsteps moving through the house and into the hallway below. The steps stopped and it sounded as if someone were trying a door. Was it Krantz, back to check on the basement? But now the steps continued down the hall and up the stairs. If it was Krantz, why wasn't he focused on the basement door? Why would he come up here? Had he seen the light of her candle glowing through the blinds? With her heart in her throat, she hoped she wasn't about to scream.

"It's me," Jon's voice called through the door.

Relief washing over her, she moved the desk away, quickly letting him in.

"Krantz was parked out there. Just sitting in his car, a couple of houses down. Too close to the rock for me to risk it." He pushed the desk back in front of the door, wincing in pain when it bumped the bandage protecting his thigh.

"How's your leg?" she asked with concern.

"Pretty sore." He frowned. "We've got to get out of here, Leah."

"I know."

"But with all these cops crawling all over the place, it won't be easy."

"Maybe we should just lay low," she suggested.

"Wait until morning and see if there's a changing of the guard. Hearing that one of the cops was mad at Krantz for breaking in here without a warrant makes me feel a tinge of hope."

"And if he does come back, he'll probably just check the basement."

"And maybe he'll be alone," she said positively.

"Let's move the bureau against the door, too," Jon suggested. "Make it extra hard for him to get in here. Just in case."

"Then we can take turns sleeping," she told him as she helped him move the heavy bureau. "You should go first since you're the one with the gunshot wound."

He started to protest this, but she wouldn't take no for an answer. As if to drive home her decision she sat in the only chair—a comfy-looking club chair—pointing to the single bed against the wall. He sat down reluctantly. "I only want to sleep an hour," he said in a weary tone. "Promise you'll wake me up, okay?"

She just nodded.

"And if you hear anything downstairs—or the alarm goes off—just nudge me."

"Isn't the alarm disarmed now?"

"I'm guessing the police called the security company to have it reset. At least that's what they're supposed to do."

"Okay. Well, get some rest."

"I'll try." He leaned back onto the pillows with his sandals still on. "Although I feel wide awake now."

"Try to relax," she said quietly. Then, seeing that the portrait was still on the floor where she'd dropped it, she went over to pick it up. "I took a sneak peek at your paintings," she admitted.

"Uh-huh."

"You're really good." She studied the portrait before returning it to the stack, leaving it face out. "I can see why you're questioning your choice of careers."

"Really?" Jon sat up and peered curiously at her.

"Absolutely."

"Well, thanks."

"And you're versatile, too," she said. "Seascapes, children. And that stunning woman." She glanced at him. "Monica?"

He nodded. "So you've met Monica."

"Monica? Is she your girlfriend?" She tried to sound nonchalant as she sat back in the club chair, tucking her legs underneath her.

"Ex." His mouth twisted to one side.

"Ex?" She studied him closely. Something about his expression wasn't convincing her.

"Monica and I parted ways last summer." He sighed and leaned back on the bed.

"She's very beautiful."

"Uh-huh."

"Did you *part ways* amicably?" she asked, knowing that it was none of her business.

"Not exactly." He frowned.

"Were you in love?" she persisted quietly.

"I *thought* we were in love." Jon closed his eyes, exhaling loudly.

"Sorry…you should go to sleep."

"It's just that she's not someone I care to think about," he said sleepily. "Moving on, you know?"

"Yeah, sure," she mumbled. But the truth was she didn't believe him. As she sat there staring into those beautiful eyes, she knew that Jon still loved her. No one could paint a portrait like that—of someone he confessed to have loved—and then just stop loving her altogether. It didn't seem possible.

Leah didn't know why this felt so disturbing to her, but it did. It felt as if that painting—as if Monica—had invaded their strange little world and just wrecked everything. Of course, she knew this was perfectly ridiculous. After all, what did she and Jon really have? Being trapped together by a madman who wanted them dead was hardly the foundation for a good relationship. And just the same, she felt so drawn to him. He was the reason she'd decided to take a beach run earlier today. Was that really just today? It felt like weeks ago.

But her hope when she'd quickly changed her clothes after her shift at The Willows had been to accidentally "bump into" that sandy-haired stranger and his little dog, Ralph. And although that had happened, it had turned into the biggest mess of her life. Not only had she endangered her own life—she'd endangered his, too.

She looked over to the green-eyed beauty watching the room with such regal tranquility. And then to discover that the woman who had probably been the love of his life looked like that. Well, it just seemed all wrong. Leah puffed out the candle and closed her eyes. She didn't plan to sleep, but she knew she needed to relax a little. And she needed to pray.

When Leah woke up it was to the sharp siren sounds of the security alarm. She got out of her chair, crawling across the floor to nudge Jon, when the sound of a loud crash made her jump. She reached over to pet Ralph, soothing him and keeping him calm and hopefully quiet. But someone had intruded. Probably Krantz.

Jon got down on the floor next to her and she could hear him fumbling for something. With his hand cupped over the beam of the flashlight, he allowed enough light in the room for him to get his hands on the baseball bat and he handed her the tire iron, signaling silence as he turned off the flashlight.

Leah could feel her heart pounding wildly as she listened to the security alarm, wondering if the intruder was coming up the stairs. She suspected it was Krantz. He'd probably kicked down the basement door to investigate down there. Hopefully they'd left nothing behind to give them away. She peered at the illuminated face of her watch, shocked to see that it was already past five in the morning. They had both slept for about four hours.

Another loud bang made her jump again, but Jon reached over to grasp her trembling hand, holding it firmly as if to warn her to keep silent. And it was a good thing because a part of her was ready to scream like a crazy person. As if the thin thread holding her sanity together was ready to break—and then she would lose it. But instead of screaming, she felt hot silent tears slipping down her cheeks. When would this madness end?

SEVEN

Jon felt certain Krantz was the intruder and although he never heard him leave, he suspected he was gone when the obnoxious alarm siren abruptly came to a stop. And yet Jon was hesitant to move. For two reasons. First and foremost, he wasn't positive that Krantz was gone. Second, he wasn't sure he could get up from the floor where they'd been sitting. His leg burned like fire, and every muscle in his body ached. And so he remained on the floor with Leah, enclosed in silence in the darkened room. His ears still ringing from the security alarm, Jon wondered if this was how it felt after an air raid.

"Krantz must've called the security company," he whispered to Leah, "to turn that alarm off."

"Uh-huh." Her voice sounded shaky, and who could blame her? Not for the first time, he thought she'd been impressively brave through all this. Not everyone could keep their cool as she'd done. Still, he knew that she had to be tired and as he turned on the flashlight, he could see the strain lines on her face.

"You okay?" he asked gently.

She just nodded.

"It's pretty unnerving," he admitted quietly.

"Yeah. Now what?" She looked at him with frightened eyes.

"We've got to get out of here—and get help—soon." He felt foolish for stating the obvious. But just because it was obvious did not make it easy.

"How?"

"I was thinking about the ATV again," he said. "At some point this morning, the police shift has got to change. Krantz has been on for at least twelve hours now. Even if he volunteered to put in overtime, I can't imagine any responsible captain letting him stay on the clock. I think our chance is coming up soon."

"But what if Krantz doesn't let up—even if his shift ends?"

"Well, it seems he'd have to turn his car in. That would get him out of here for a while...don't you think?"

"I guess so."

"So I've been trying to concoct a plan."

"Yes?"

"As soon as it seems like the cops are gone, we'll drive the ATV down to the jetty. But from there, we'll have to hoof it. It'll be a rough hike for about a mile, but once we reach the beach road, it's only a couple miles to town—and the phone should get some connectivity even before we get to town."

"That sounds doable." Her eyes lit up with hope.

"Yeah..." He frowned at his bandaged leg. "And even if I couldn't make it all the way, you should be able to get there without me, Leah." He grimaced. "You might even have a better chance on your own. Make better time anyway."

"I can't just leave you behind." She looked at him with such tenderness that he felt a catch in his throat. "We're in this together, Jon." She placed a gentle hand on his shoulder, sending a warm feeling rushing through him—almost enough to camouflage the pain surging through his leg.

"I'd be okay if you went on ahead," he assured her. "I'd just lie low somewhere. You could send help for me later. It might be our only chance, Leah."

She frowned. "Well, I guess we'll have to see how it goes." She brightened. "But what if we came to a house where someone was home—couldn't we stop to use a landline phone?"

"Remember what we heard on the radio last night, Leah—anyone who's listened to the news will still think we're dangerous wanted criminals. They'd probably slam the door in our faces and call the police. Too risky."

"Oh, yeah."

"And once we get on the road, we'll really have to watch for traffic. We'll have to hide if we see anyone around—not just cops."

"Right."

She reached over to his bandaged thigh, gently pressing down a loose edge of adhesive tape. "Do you really think you can walk okay—for up to three miles and parts on rough terrain?"

"I'm not sure." He frowned. "I hate to admit it, but it hurts a lot more today."

"I was worried about that."

"I feel like I've been hit by a truck," he confessed.

"Not surprising. I should probably replace your bandage and—"

"I don't think we should waste the time." He reached over to where Ralph was just sitting up in bed. "How you doing, old boy?"

"Should he have another tranquilizer?" she asked. "In case Krantz comes back?"

"I think he'll be okay." He scratched Ralph's ear.

"He really does seem pretty laid-back. I hadn't gotten that impression when he'd gone after Krantz." She smiled. "But he was trying to be a hero."

"My mom originally got Ralph for me," he confessed. "She thought I was lonely and could use a dog. When I declined the offer, she kept him instead. So I guess he's sort of mine. Going after Krantz was out of character for him. He usually is even-tempered and quiet. He must have wanted to protect you."

"He's a sweet dog."

"I'll go see about the ATV now. I'll do a quick cop-check while I'm down there. I really think our chance to get out of here is imminent."

"Sure." She stiffly got to her feet, groaning as if her muscles were aching, too.

"And we should eat something." He used the side of the club chair to pull himself to his feet.

"And have some fluids." She picked up a water bottle from one of the boxes they'd hauled up there the previous night.

Jon poked around in another box. "I don't think there's much food left from last night up here, but I'll bring something up from the kitchen when I come back."

"Be careful," she warned him as he pushed the desk away from the door. "It'll be daylight soon."

"That light should work in our favor as far as hiding in the house. We can see out better than they can see in now. And it won't be so easy for cops to look into the garage while I'm gassing up the ATV."

"And you know that the ATV works?" she asked.

"I'm going to find out." He attempted a brave smile. "Say a prayer."

She nodded with a genuine expression. "Believe me, I will. I honestly think that prayer is about all we have going for us right now."

He hated to admit it, but he thought she was right. The chances of getting the old ATV to start up without a hitch seemed small. Still, it was worth a try.

After Jon left, Leah lit the candle, then she poured from her water bottle into Ralph's bowl, urging him to drink. While he lapped at it, she dug through the boxes until she found a can of dog food and coaxed him to eat. Although the dog had relieved himself in the basement last night, he didn't seem to be wanting out now. Not that she could do much about it anyway. And she suspected he'd be safest if he were confined to this room. She'd put some paper down for him.

"Come on, little guy," she said. "Eat up. Your body needs the nutrition." While she waited for him to eat, hoping a full tummy would help make him sleepy, she dug out the radio, turning it on with the volume so low that it was barely audible. The music, though not her favorite style, was comforting. Plus it was a good distraction.

After Ralph finished the food, she picked him up and gently held him in her lap. She wasn't sure who was most soothed by this, but as she stroked his wiry brown coat, she felt herself relaxing ever so slightly.

The radio was tuned to the same station her mom used to listen to—back before Alzheimer's had started taking over. Leah remembered how she'd sometimes teased her mom for listening to the oldies. What she wouldn't give for Mom to even recognize these old tunes now—or sing along to the lyrics the way she used to. Occasionally Mom would hear a song and it would register with her for a few moments—but like the morning fog, it would fade away. And for the most part, she seemed like an alien…a stranger who was lost in a foreign world.

Kind of how Leah felt right now. As if everything familiar had been ripped away from her—turned upside down. As if anything and everything was a potential threat. Well, except for Jon. Having him around made a huge difference. Leah couldn't even imagine how she would've handled all this if Jon hadn't been with her. Or what she'd do if anything happened to him. She held her breath for a moment, intently listening, but hearing only the sound of the waves and the radio playing quietly. She assumed the silence of the house below meant that all was well. At least for the moment.

She prayed for him, praying that he'd be safe. And that the ATV would start—praying that it wouldn't make noise to draw anyone's attention and that Jon would have the right mechanical skills to get it going.

She thought about Jon down there working on the ATV. She liked the fact that, even though he was an attorney, he still knew how to fix things. She'd been impressed that he'd been rebuilding his carburetor—that he could work with his hands. She'd never told anyone this before, but she'd always dreamed that she'd marry someone who knew how to fix things. Oh, she didn't want that to be all they could do, but not having had a dad at home—and having seen too many things go unfixed—it had seemed important to her. A childish secret that she'd kept for years. In the short time she'd known Jon, she'd observed many admirable qualities. The sort of traits she would appreciate in a husband.

Not that she expected Jon to propose marriage to her! She might be feeling slightly crazed over the recent chaotic upheaval in her life, but she wasn't delusional. For sure, she'd felt an instant attraction to this guy— one that seemed to go both ways—but under the circumstances, well, it was a little hard to actually know if it was real or not.

As she scratched behind Ralph's ears, she vaguely wondered about Stockholm Syndrome…but wasn't that when victims fell for their captors? Jon was hardly her captor. If anything, he'd gotten into this mess by trying to help her. It warmed her heart to remember how he'd jumped to her rescue. But in the next instant, a chill went through her as she remembered how Krantz had attempted to kill Jon. And how Krantz probably wouldn't back off until they were both dead—or locked behind bars.

She took in a deep breath, trying to calm herself again as she focused on Ralph and the quiet music from the radio. A song her mom used to love was playing now. Something about Mona Lisa's smile. Leah turned the volume up a hair to hear it better, trying to make out the lyrics of the slightly haunting tune. But as she listened to someone singing about a "lovely work of art," her attention shifted to the disturbing portrait. Monica's beautiful image was still face forward, leaned against the other canvases. And she seemed even more stunning today than she had been last night.

Leah imagined Jon painting this portrait...and the love he must've been feeling as he captured the image of this woman. She'd sensed those strong emotions in his charcoal sketches of her, too. She'd suspected from the get-go that Monica was more than just an attractive subject. And, despite feeling foolish for it, Leah had felt jealous about it. Oh, it made no sense. It wasn't as if she and Jon were a couple—although she wished they could be. She could imagine them together—under different circumstances. But knowing he'd had this other woman in his life—this gorgeous woman—well, that just seemed to put the kibosh on the whole idea.

His reply when she'd asked him about Monica last night hadn't exactly been encouraging. She'd hoped he'd say something like, "Oh, she was just a friend who modeled for me. No big deal." Or perhaps he'd say she was his sister, although he hadn't mentioned a sister. Instead, his answers had seemed vague—intentionally vague—which gave her the impression that he still had feelings for her. And, really, why was she thinking about all this now? Here she was in a life-and-death situation, and she was worrying about some woman in a painting?

Seeing that Ralph was nearly asleep, she gently laid him in the crate. Then she went over and put the portrait of Monica back where it belonged—behind the others as it had been when she'd found it. Some stones really were better left unturned. As she sat down in the club chair, she heard the local news coming on, signifying the top of the hour. And sure enough, it was 6:00 a.m.

"We have breaking news in Cape Perpetua," the newscaster began. She listened as he repeated the same information from last night about the "assault on a police officer and possible drug cartel couple on the lam." Although this time he compared Leah and Jon to Bonnie and Clyde, which seemed a pretty gigantic leap. The news folks probably enjoyed sensationalizing the whole thing.

"In the latest breaking news update, which police have linked to the wanted couple, a woman from The Willows assisted living facility is reported as missing."

Leah gasped as she picked up the radio, holding it closer to hear.

"Leah Hampton was a part-time employee at The Willows. According to facility manager Barb Glasner, Miss Hampton's mother, Ellen Hampton, is a patient in the nursing-care section. The fifty-two-year-old reportedly went missing early this morning. Police suspect that Leah Hampton and her unidentified companion are responsible for Ellen Hampton's disappearance from the care facility." The newscaster quoted Barb Glasner again, claiming that only someone with insider information, *like an employee*, would be able to sneak a patient out unobserved.

"Anyone who has seen, or has any information, regarding the whereabouts of Leah Hampton or Ellen Hampton or the as-yet-unidentified male are urged to contact local authorities at once. As we remind our listeners, these two criminals are considered extremely dangerous. Do not approach or engage with them. Call 911 if you see them." This was followed by full physical descriptions of all three of them and the insinuation that Leah's mother would be at physical risk if she was with her daughter and her dangerous friend as suspected.

Leah's heart pounded in her throat as she absorbed this horrific news. Where was her mother? How could she have gone missing? She felt outraged to think that the police were blaming her for putting her mother in danger. That wasn't just a flat-out lie, it was certifiably nuts! Leah had spent the last two years devoting her life to her mother, doing all she could to keep her mother in a good care facility and even working there part-time to help with the expenses.

Krantz had to be behind this somehow. *But how?* And why on earth would he want to kidnap a poor sick woman suffering from Alzheimer's? What did he possibly hope to gain from that?

Before she could even begin to answer this question, she heard loud footsteps clumping up the stairs. She turned off the radio and listened as the heavy steps drew closer and then, before she could do anything, Ralph jumped out of his box and, despite her attempt to hush him, started barking at the door—the door she had neglected to barricade with the desk and bureau. And now it was too late!

EIGHT

Leah felt dizzy with fear as she cowered behind the club chair, waiting for the door to burst open—the perpetrator to enter. But instead there was a quiet knocking, followed by Jon's voice, identifying himself.

"Come in," she called out weakly. "It's open."

"I'm surprised you didn't barricade it." Jon entered the room with a bag in hand, then paused to peer closely at her. "Are you okay?"

"I don't know." She took in a deep breath, sinking back into the chair.

He set the bag on the desk, staring at her with a furrowed brow. "You look pale, Leah. You're not sick, are you?"

"No…" Although she did feel slightly sick as she pulled her knees up to her chest, fighting off the urge to sob uncontrollably. "I'm just really scared." She shook her head, still trying to figure this thing with her mother out.

"What happened?"

"It just keeps getting worse, Jon. Worse and worse."

Jon came over, putting a hand on her shoulder. "What's wrong?" he asked.

So, trying not to cry, she explained the news on the radio.

"Your mother's gone missing?" He sounded incredulous.

She barely nodded. "Early this morning."

"Do you think she might've wandered off? I had a grandmother with senility issues. She did that occasionally. My dad finally had to put her in a home."

"Mom's *never* wandered off before," Leah told him. "There are some Alzheimer's patients who do that all the time, but my mom has never been a flight risk. *Never.*"

"Oh."

"This is related to Krantz. I just know it." She pounded her fist into the arm of the chair. "He's behind it."

"But how?" Jon sat on the edge of the bed. "I thought he was around here most of the night."

"But how do you *know* that?" she demanded. "We were both asleep—how could we possible know where Krantz was?" Once again, she wondered why she hadn't just slipped out and attempted to run to town last night. Sure, it was more than ten miles, but she'd been training for a marathon. Ten miles wasn't much—not if she'd taken the main road. Except for the armed policemen that might've tried to shoot her. There was that. "We don't know what Krantz was up to last night. Not while we were sleeping."

"Yeah...good point." Jon rubbed his chin with a puzzled expression.

"Krantz might've left—gone to town. Maybe his

shift ended and we didn't even know it. He could've gone over to The Willows and kidnapped my mom while we were sleeping." She could hear the tinge of hysteria in her voice—she knew that wouldn't help anything. And it wasn't as if it were Jon's fault. She had to calm down, to think clearly. But how?

"But *why* would he do that, Leah?"

"Why would he do *any* of this?" she demanded. "None of this makes sense."

"Yeah, that's true. But how would Krantz even know your mom was there?"

Leah had already considered this. "Krantz had access to my car—and my purse was in there. My employee ID card for The Willows would've been right on top, along with all my other personal information— address on my license, friends in my phone—Krantz probably has all of it in his grimy hands right now." This thought alone made her feel like throwing up.

"Even so. How would he know your mom was there at the nursing home, Leah? And, more than that, why would he kidnap her?"

"Maybe he went to The Willows to question them about me," she suggested. "You know, since I'm a dangerous wanted criminal." She cringed to think of Barb hearing this from a policeman. Would she believe it? Or would she defend Leah's character? "Maybe someone working there mentioned my mom to Krantz. Maybe he saw his opportunity and just took it."

"But isn't there good security there? Cameras and whatnot?"

"Yes." Leah bit into her lip. "But Krantz is a cop, he's

familiar with that stuff. Maybe he knew how to over-
ride the system somehow—*I don't know.*" She held up
her hands. "All I know is *my mom is missing.*" A painful lump was building in her throat and her eyes were
burning.

"But I still don't get why, Leah."

"To get to me," Leah declared, blinking back tears.
"Krantz wants to shut me up or draw me out or something. He'll use my mom to do it. I just know it. And
my mom is in serious danger right now. And there's
nothing I can do about it. At least not from here." She
looked desperately around the small room, suddenly
seeing it as a prison cell.

Jon slowly nodded. "Yeah… I guess I can see how
Krantz might think that. It's possible he kidnapped your
mom." Even so, his brow looked skeptical.

"I know it sounds crazy," she blurted, "this whole
thing is crazy."

"But even if Krantz did kidnap her, how would he
expect you to hear about it?"

She shook her fists in the air. "I *have* heard about it!
Somehow he must've known that I would. That I'd listen
to the news—or someone would tell me. And I'm sure
he thinks that it'll draw me out." She slammed her fists
into the chair arms. "And of course, I *want* to protect
my mom. Even if I have to make myself known to do
it. And that's when he plans to grab me." She pointed
at Jon. "And he probably hopes to get you, too."

"I guess that makes sense." But he still looked a little doubtful.

"I know it sounds moronic." Leah locked eyes with

Jon. "But I feel more certain than ever that Krantz is involved in human trafficking."

"I know." He nodded. "I'm having similar suspicions."

"And it might just be a gut feeling, but I think your mom had it, too. That has to be why Krantz stopped me yesterday, why he was taking me into so-called custody. He was kidnapping me the same way he kidnapped those two girls—and who knows how many others. He's a monster. And now he's taken my mom, too—*I just know it!*" Leah broke into sobs.

Jon came over and gathered her into his arms. "She's going to be okay," he said soothingly. "Krantz will keep your mom alive in order to get to us. He wants her as leverage. So he won't hurt her, Leah. But you're right. We've got to get out of here. We need to get help."

Leah blinked through her tears. "Jon, do you think that warehouse—the one your mom took the photo of—do you think that's really where the human-trafficking ring hides them? Maybe like a holding tank or something? Do you think that maybe my mom could be there right now?"

"I don't know, but if we can get out of here—if we don't get caught, we'll set the authorities onto it. As soon as we can. Maybe this morning."

"Does the ATV work?" she asked eagerly.

"Yes. And as soon as it looks like the changing of the guard out there—soon as we get a break from those patrol cars, we will be taking off." Jon pointed to her watch. "What time is it now?"

"Almost six-thirty."

"Eat something." Jon handed her a box of ginger-snaps and a bottle of apple juice. "Sorry, the provisions down there were getting skimpy."

"I'm not really hungry."

"Then stick some things in your pockets. And at least drink the juice. I'm going downstairs to keep watch. As soon as it looks like they've gone, we have to head out of here. And we have to do it fast. My guess is that their shift change is either seven or eight. We need to be ready to roll—okay?"

"What about Ralph?" Leah took a small bite of a cookie, shoving a few others into the pockets of her hoodie before taking a swig of juice.

"We don't have any choice but to leave him here. I think he'll be safer here than with us."

"I'll fill his water dish, and I'll leave some food for him, too."

"Come down as soon as you're ready," Jon told her. "I'll be in the front room. I have a feeling there's no time to waste."

Leah filled the water and food bowls, then tucked a towel around Ralph, whispering a quick safety prayer for him before she hurried downstairs. After a bathroom break, she rummaged through the hamper and found her slightly damp running clothes, which she slipped on beneath the purple warm-ups. Just in case. Then she crept across the front room floor to join Jon, who was hunkered down on the sofa, peering out the window.

"Any sign of life out there?" she whispered.

"A couple of cop cars just passed by here, like, three

minutes ago. Not far apart. Headed south. But Krantz's unmarked vehicle wasn't with them."

"Where do you think he is?"

"Maybe you're right. Maybe he went to town and kidnapped your mom." Jon frowned. "Maybe he's stashing her somewhere right now."

She took in a sharp breath. "We have to get out of here."

He nodded grimly. "So I'm guessing the cruisers will turn around at the end of the road. They should be doubling back in a couple minutes. Then they'll pass this way again."

"And then?"

"And then we'll hope and pray their shift is ending, that they'll be heading to the police station."

"And if not?"

He sighed. "Well, I'm guessing they'll continue cruising down the whole row of beach houses. That alone should buy us time. According to my estimations, we ought to be able to make it nearly to the jetty before they even get back here." He slipped off the sofa, still keeping low. "Let's go to the garage and be ready to go."

"Okay." Staying low, she followed him out to the garage. There, she saw that he'd already positioned the green ATV up close to the garage door. It looked ready to go.

"There's only one helmet." He handed her a black helmet.

"You're the driver," she said, pushing it back.

He shook his head with a stubborn expression. "You wear it or else."

Knowing it was useless to argue, she strapped it on, wondering if it were bulletproof.

"You stand here." He pointed to the garage door opener near the door. "Stay out of sight and keep watch. As soon as you see them both go past again, let me know, and when they're out of view, push the opener and I'll get the ATV to the driveway."

"Right."

"As soon as the ATV's outside, and no one's around, you hit that button to close the door and jump on the back." He explained how to avoid tripping the safety stop on the door. "And make it fast." He got onto the ATV now, hunkered down low so that no one could see him through the window.

Like a sentry, she watched out the corner of the window until she saw the first police cruiser coming down the road. "Car number one," she said quietly. She waited and before long the second car came slowly along. "Car number two." As the second car disappeared from sight, she pushed the button. As the door opened, she stepped under it and out to the driveway, peering down the road to be sure they weren't returning.

The ATV's motor was louder than she expected and she hoped the cops' windows weren't down to hear the noise. As soon as Jon pulled into the driveway, she hit the garage door button, then sprinted out to join him. Climbing on behind Jon, she peered over his shoulder, looking down the road to see if the cars had turned back.

"Hold on tight," Jon commanded as he took off down

the road. "The beach access is a few houses down. When I leave the road, the ride will be rough."

She wrapped her arms around his waist, clinging tightly. "How fast can this thing go?"

"Eighty at tops."

She gulped and, thankful for the helmet, held on tight. Before long, he turned off the road and started down a steep and bumpy beach-access trail that was not designed for vehicles. Holding her breath, she looked down toward the beach. The tide was out, and what little she could see looked empty. Hopefully it would be completely deserted—at least free of cops.

Jon seemed to know what he was doing as he skillfully maneuvered the bulky vehicle down the rough terrain and, after a few more big lumps and bumps, they were on the level beach and Leah was able to breathe again.

"We'll make better time on the wet packed sand," he told her above the noise of the engine. "But we'll be more visible out there, too."

"Why not stay in the soft stuff for a while?" she yelled back. "Just to stay out of sight of the bluff. In case the cops heard the engine noise."

"Good idea."

And so he ran the ATV alongside the shaded area of the bluff, zigzagging a maze of driftwood and oversize rocks. But they weren't putting much distance behind them. Feeling nervous that they weren't making good time, Leah turned around to peer back, making sure they weren't being followed. No one was there, but still feeling a wave of anxiety, she called out again. "Maybe we should go for speed instead!"

"Yeah." He nodded. "That's what I'm thinking. *Hold on!*" And now he turned out toward the ocean. Soon he was running the ATV through the wet sand, going at a much higher speed. She had no idea how fast he was going, but everything was whizzing by. And, trying not to remember some of the ATV accident victims she'd cared for while doing her practicum at the local hospital last semester, Leah held on tighter.

After a minute or so, she relaxed just a little. And instead of obsessing over broken bones and brain injuries, she prayed—still clinging tightly to Jon. And she didn't mind the feeling of being this close to him. He felt firm and strong and capable. She knew she could get used to this—under different circumstances. And despite the uncomfortable speed and knowing they were still in danger, she felt a faint smidgen of hope. Maybe they were going to escape this thing alive.

As the jetty came in sight, probably just a couple of miles away, she felt a happy rush—they were going to make it! Feeling almost giddy with confidence, she turned to look over her shoulder, and in that same instant, she nearly lost it.

"Jon!" she screamed. "Krantz's car! Less than a mile behind us!"

"Hold on," he yelled.

She tightened her grasp and leaned into him as the ATV lurch forward, going even faster. Laying her helmeted head against his back in the hopes it would make them more aerodynamic, she prayed for safety.

"Creek ahead," Jon yelled to her. "Gonna be rough!"

"Okay!" she yelled back.

As they bounced and splashed through the creek, she heard the sharp sound of gunshots. Bracing herself for the pain of a bullet—or worse—she buried her face into Jon's back and prayed even harder.

"We're going up the dunes," Jon yelled as he slowed down to turn inland.

She looked to where he was heading, staring in horror at the hill of sand that looked almost perpendicular to the beach. Could the ATV possibly climb that slope without toppling? And even if the vehicle could hold on, wouldn't they become an even easier target?

Afraid to breathe, she stared ahead in terror as they started to climb, wondering which would hurt more—broken bones or gunshot wounds. She could feel her fingers digging into Jon's ribs, trying to hold on as he pushed the ATV even higher—the sounds of bullets from behind.

"We're gonna jump for it," he yelled as the top came into sight. "Don't let go of me. We go uphill. The ATV goes down."

"Okay!" she yelled back, processing this plan. And clinging to him for her life, she watched as he released his hold on the ATV, throwing himself to the left. In that same moment, she hoisted herself along with him. Somehow they went upward into the dune—while gravity sucked the ATV down the hill. As it tumbled, more shots rang out.

NINE

"Come on." Jon grabbed her hand, pulling her to her feet as she scrambled in the loose sand. Kicking herself into high gear, she lunged upward so fast that she was actually tugging him. Without pausing and still hearing gunshots, they scrambled to the top of the dune, gunshots ringing out again as they dove over it, tumbling down the other side in a flurry of arms and legs and sand. Landing just short of a smelly bog of rancid water, Leah jumped to her feet, extending a helping hand to Jon.

He pointed to the nearby pine trees. "Let's head there for cover."

Still clasping hands, they ran toward the wooded area. Leah knew Krantz couldn't climb that steep dune in his car, and if he tried to scale it on foot, it would be a while before he caught up with them. Just the same, she wanted as much space between them and him as possible.

"This way." Jon tugged on her hand, pulling in the opposite direction.

"I thought we were going to the jetty."

"We will. But if someone tracks us from the beach, or if a helicopter comes by, our footprints through this open area will point north. Maybe they'll think we cut across the wetland area—to get to the road."

"Right." She ran alongside him. "But anyone familiar with that terrain knows it's a stupid way to go. You could be lost in that mess for days."

"Yeah," he said breathlessly. "Maybe they'll think we're stupid."

She knew he was right to make a faux trail, but she also knew by his limp that his leg was hurting. Any extra steps would probably end up costing them…eventually. When they reached the shelter of the trees, they turned back toward south—toward the jetty, but staying within the tree shadows.

"How far to the jetty?" she asked as they slowed down to an easy jog.

"Couple miles," he huffed.

That would've been her guess, too. And two miles was nothing for her. She glanced at him, noticing how his injured leg seemed to be dragging. She purposely slowed the pace down. If they could just make it to the jetty, there might be a good place for him to hide around there. If he could just make it. At the moment, she wasn't sure he could.

After about twenty minutes, they had slowed down to a fast walk. Even that seemed to be taxing for Jon. "Are you okay?" she asked.

"My leg's not too good." He wiped his hand across his brow. "Sorry to slow us down. Maybe you should go without me—"

"No," she insisted. "Not until we get to the jetty and find you a good place to hide."

"Hope I can last that long."

"You can," she assured him. "And we probably don't have to go fast. I really doubt Krantz would give up his car and try to follow us up the hill."

"Probably not. But he knows we're up here. Might send a helicopter."

"But they can't see us in the trees."

"Yeah." Jon nodded.

"Even if they saw us, they probably wouldn't shoot— if we held up our hands to surrender," she said. "Well, unless Krantz was with them. He'd probably shoot, but fortunately, he's a bad shot."

"It probably wasn't easy to drive and shoot at the same time. But I think you're right. He's a bad shot."

"That's good news for us."

"Especially since it sounded like he was using his high-powered rifle."

"What's that?" Leah pointed to a wide path that cut into the landscape up ahead.

"Looks like some kind of a road."

"Out here?"

"Maybe it's a logging road," Jon suggested as they paused to survey the strip of packed sand and dirt.

"But this is a protected area," she pointed out.

"Yeah, that's what I thought, too." He leaned over to peer down at the road—or maybe to catch his breath. "And a road back in here's illegal."

"Maybe it's an old road from before it was designated a wetland." Even as she said this, it seemed unlikely.

She knew how fast vegetation grew around here. An unused road could get covered up in just a few years.

He knelt down to look closely at the road's surface. "These are tire tracks," he said quietly. "Fresh, too."

"Maybe it's from a forest ranger's vehicle." She felt a chill run through her as she remembered the contents of the folder. "Or maybe this road leads to that warehouse—the one your mom photographed."

He nodded with a furrowed brow. "That's what I was just thinking."

"Should we follow it?"

"I'd like to see where it goes." He pointed away from the road, back into the trees. "From a safe distance. Just in case."

"Yeah."

Although it wasn't as easy to walk through the brushy woods, Leah felt thankful for the cover of the trees. If that road really did lead to the warehouse— and if that warehouse really was a place to imprison kidnapped victims—this path could be very dangerous. Lethal.

"Do you think your dad's ATV survived the crash?" she asked quietly, just trying to make conversation, to keep her mind off what might lie ahead.

"ATVs are pretty tough. It'll probably be okay. With a little mechanical work." He reached out to help her step over a fallen log.

"Unless Krantz messes with it." She could imagine Krantz pulling out his guns and shooting the ATV to pieces just for revenge—that is if he could hit it. The image was almost laughable. Except that it wasn't.

Jon grimly shook his head. "Krantz isn't going to keep getting away with his lawlessness forever," he said with determination. "He will eventually get caught. He'll get what's coming to him."

"What makes you so sure?" she asked with genuine curiosity. She wanted to add, how did he know that Krantz wouldn't catch up with both of them, shoot them dead and bury them in a shallow grave—and get away with it? Or maybe Jon was talking about something beyond this life. "How do you know Krantz will eventually get caught?"

"I left a note in my dad's desk—in his secret drawer. I wrote down all the details of this nightmare. I put my mom's file about human trafficking with it, too."

"Oh…?"

"Just in case."

"In case we don't make it out of this…alive?"

He made a crooked smile, reaching over to pluck a pine needle from her hair. "We'll make it out alive, Leah."

"I want to believe that."

Jon waved a hand. "Hey, just look how far we've come already." He stopped walking, pausing to unbutton one of the pockets of his cargo pants and extracting his phone, checking it then putting it back. "I figured my phone wouldn't have any connectivity yet." Now he removed a stainless-steel compass. "This is my backup plan."

"Good idea." She studied his bulky-looking cargo pants as he got their bearings. "What else you got in those pockets?"

He made a lopsided grin as he slipped the compass into a higher pocket and they continued to walk. "Some things I thought we might need." He began to list some random items, including matches, string, wire, a Swiss Army knife and a few other things.

"Were you a Boy Scout or something?"

"No. My dad loved this old TV show called *Mac-Gyver*. I used to watch reruns of it with him as a kid. Then Dad and I would go on exploratory hikes and put some of our MacGyver skills to use."

"Your parents sound pretty cool."

"They are." His brown eyes shone warmly as he smiled. "You'd like them, Leah. And they'd like you, too." He patted her on the back. "You're a real can-do kinda girl."

"Thanks."

Just then he stumbled on some underbrush, making a rough landing on his bad leg. As she helped him back up, she felt bad that she hadn't insisted on replacing his dressing. Maybe the wound was worse than she'd thought yesterday. Or maybe it was infected. Whatever the case, she knew he was in pain.

"Let's take a break." She pointed to a nearby fallen log. Far enough from the road that they'd never be noticed if a vehicle happened by.

Jon seemed glad to agree to this and after they sat down, he extracted a water bottle and energy bar from one of his cargo pants pockets. For a couple minutes, they just sat there in the silence of the woods, sharing the water and granola bar between them.

"I really hope you get to meet my parents...someday," Jon said as he tucked the wrapper of the bar into a pocket.

"Someday," she echoed absently, as if she didn't really think he meant it.

"I didn't mean it like that," he said quickly. "I meant *someday* when we get out of this mess. Someday when my parents get back from their cruise."

"Oh…?" She studied him, trying to discern what he was really saying. "Well, I'd like to meet them, too. They sound very interesting."

He tipped his head to one side. "And that sounded like a very polite way of saying you're really not interested."

She blinked. "No, that's not true."

"I know I already asked you, Leah, if there's a guy in your life. A boyfriend or fiancé or someone and I'm pretty sure you said you were single. Right?"

She nodded. "Absolutely. I've been so busy these past couple of years. Trying to finish my RN degree. Doing practicum in the hospital. Working part-time at The Willows. And before that, I was taking care of my mom. And I sort of help with my great-aunt. On top of all that, I made it a goal to complete a marathon before I turn twenty-five. And, trust me, time's a-wasting on that one."

He smiled. "I've no doubt you can pull it off."

"So, honestly, I've been too busy for a relationship. I can't even remember the last time I had a real date." She narrowed her eyes slightly. "Unlike *you*."

"Huh?"

"You and *Monica*." She made a little smirk. "I'm

sure you can remember the last date you had with her."
Okay, she knew she was being nosy and snarky and incredibly rude, but she just wanted to know.

"It's been a while."

"Really? How long?" She studied him closely.

His brow creased. "About a year, I guess. Like I told you, Leah. That's over."

"That's what you say with your lips." She slowly stood up, knowing they should keep moving. Especially before his muscles started to tighten up. "But I think your paintbrush tells another story." She grinned as she reached for his hand, pulling him to his feet.

"And I think that you've got a very good imagination."

She shrugged and, without saying another word, she turned around and began picking her way through the woods again. She could hear him moving behind her and she considered continuing their conversation, but really, what more was there to say? Jon could pretend that it was over between him and Monica, but Leah had a strong sense that it was not. And maybe she did have a good imagination, but it all seemed clear to her.

The mysterious Monica had somehow, for some unknowable reason, broken Jon's heart. It was the only thing that made sense to Leah. It explained his hesitancy to talk about this gorgeous woman, and the reason he portrayed her so exquisitely. And Leah suspected that if Monica came to her senses—and she should in time—she would figure out what a catch Jon was and come running back to him. It seemed as plain as day. The intelligent, handsome, artistic attorney marries the beautiful woman he's in love with—and everyone lives happily ever after. Well, everyone except Leah. But that was another story.

Suddenly Leah was brought back to the present by something that felt off. Ahead of her, barely visible through the thick trees, she noticed a dark, tall and somewhat foreboding image. And the road seemed to be leading right to it—the warehouse from the photo!

"Jon," she whispered as she turned around to grab his arm. *"Look."*

He stopped walking and, following her gaze through the trees, barely nodded. Then, holding a forefinger to his lips, he continued forward. Leading them closer, he took his time, carefully picking his way almost soundlessly through the brushy woods. With a wildly pounding heart, she imitated him.

If Jon's mother's hunches and Leah's gut feelings were correct, this place was more than just a little dangerous—this place was the reason Krantz wanted them dead. And now they had actually found it—seen it with their own eyes. And everything about it looked evil. Creepiness just seemed to seep from it, and a part of Leah wanted to turn and run the other way. Except for her worst fear—what if her mother was in there?

Keeping a cautious distance, they slowly inched closer to the building. When they got near enough, they could see that the mud-colored boxlike brown structure was completely barricaded by a tall chain-link fence. Atop the fence was curling razor wire—like around a prison yard. In the front of the windowless building was a solid-looking metal door with not just one, but two dead bolt locks. Not too far from the door was a portable outhouse, also painted a dirty brown. Leah and Jon exchanged uneasy glances.

"Stay low," Jon whispered as he crouched down, pulling her with him. "Who knows how good those security cams are. Someone could be watching us right now."

"What should we do?" she whispered back in desperation.

"I'm not sure." He glanced over to the road, then back to the building.

"Do you think anyone's inside?"

"Hard to say."

Her chest tightened as she thought of her easily confused mother. "Do you think my mom could be in there?"

He frowned. "I was just—" But before he could finish, the sound of a vehicle tearing down the road got their attention.

"Get low." He pulled them both to the ground, into the thick undergrowth of huckleberry and salal plants. From between the green vegetation, they both peered toward the building, watching as the dark car pulled up to the gated section of the fence.

Leah felt only mild surprise to see it was Krantz's unmarked police car. He got out with his revolver in hand, looking sinister. He was no longer dressed in a uniform, but was wearing dark clothing. He surveyed the surrounding area with an intensity that sent an icy chill down her spine—as if he *knew* they were nearby. She almost expected him to start shooting into the trees just to frighten them. To her relief, he didn't. Instead he hurriedly unlocked the gate and entered the compound. With the revolver still in hand, his eyes darting all around, he locked it back up again. Then, giving one long last look all around, he headed over to the building, unlocked the two dead bolts and went inside, closing the metal door with a loud clang.

"What do we do?" Leah whispered.

"Wait," Jon said quietly. "Until he leaves."

"What if he *doesn't* leave?"

Jon frowned. "He will. Eventually."

"What is he doing in there?" It made her sick to imagine that creep in there with her poor mother—and she felt certain her mom was in there.

After what felt like about an hour, but according to her watch was less than ten minutes, Krantz emerged from the building. But he was pulling someone out with him. Leah nearly gasped audibly, but somehow controlled herself. Krantz had her mother in tow. Ellen Hampton was still dressed in her favorite pink-and-white flannel pajamas, which were dirty and ripped on one knee. Her short dishwater-blond hair was messy and wild-looking, but it was her terrified expression that sliced through Leah like a jagged knife. She looked fragile and helpless as Krantz dragged her out by one arm, holding her out in front of him like a hunter who'd bagged his prey.

"I know you're out there!" Krantz yelled so loudly that her mom shrieked and the chirping birds in the trees grew silent. "If you don't show yourselves right now, I'm gonna kill her." With his free hand, he pointed his revolver at Leah's mother's head. Meanwhile she cowered in fear, sobbing like a small child. "Gonna blow her brains out."

Leah's heart was breaking, her every muscle tensed, ready to leap—ready to offer to exchange herself for her mom's safety, but Jon's hand remained firmly on her shoulder. Like a heavy anchor, he was holding her down. With a serious expression, he locked eyes with her, firmly shaking his head no, mouthing the word *wait.*

In Jon's other hand was his phone. Hidden by the shadows, it was aimed directly at the compound and in recording mode. Of course, being an attorney, he was trying to acquire evidence—and that was good. But all she cared about was her mother's safety. And as much as she knew Jon was right to lie low for now, everything in her wanted to throw caution to the wind and run to her mother's aid.

But, really, what could she do? Krantz couldn't be trusted. He would probably shoot her on sight—which would further horrify her mother—and then, of course, he would kill her mom next. Leah bit into her lip, allowing the pain to seep into her like a sedative as she remained hidden in the brush silently praying—make that *pleading*—for help.

TEN

Jon knew that Leah was about to jump out of her skin. He could feel her tensed muscles, her shaky breathing. He saw the animallike fear in her eyes. But to expose themselves right now would be suicidal. He knew that in his gut. And in the event Krantz should catch them—and Jon knew this was a possibility—Jon would have to remember to toss his smartphone into the brush in the hopes that someone would discover it later and learn the truth. Even if it was too late for him and Leah. And her poor mom.

Jon's thigh was on fire. He wasn't sure if infection had set in or if it had been more damaged than they'd assumed last night. All he knew for sure was that he wasn't going to make it to the jetty. And now that they knew Leah's mom was here, he wasn't even sure he wanted to leave. Except that they needed help.

Krantz yelled some more nasty threats—more evidence that Jon collected on his phone. This thug was clearly feeling desperate. But his desperation just made him more dangerous. For a moment, Jon considered surrendering himself in exchange for Leah's mom's safety.

But he knew that Krantz would simply take him hostage along with the frightened woman. And he felt certain that Krantz would not hesitate to kill him. Unless he thought Jon was leverage, too.

Before Jon could come to a conclusion on this idea, Krantz yanked Leah's mother back into the warehouse, slamming the door angrily behind him.

"I've got to help her," Leah whispered in a terrified tone. Despite all they'd been through together, this was the most frightened he'd seen her—and it cut him to the core.

"I have an idea," he said quietly. "You stay hidden, and when Krantz comes out, I'll offer myself in exchange for your mom's safety."

"You know he'll just kill you, Jon."

"Maybe not." He looked into her eyes. "If I can convince him that I'm more important to you than your mother—maybe he'll be motivated to keep me alive for a while."

"Why?"

He could feel himself making this up as he went, but if it kept Leah safe, maybe it didn't matter. If only one of them could survive, it had to be her. With his eyes fixed on the warehouse door, he continued, talking quietly—trying to be convincing, almost like presenting a case in court.

"I'll surrender myself. I'll explain that I'm crippled and I'll act like I'm really sorry about all this, like I have no idea what's going on with the trafficking business. Like I think he's a trustworthy cop and I was just trying to protect you. I'll tell Krantz that you're on your way into town. I'll say that you have my phone, which you will have. I'll tell him that he can contact you by phone and that he can tell you he's got me—and he can even put me on the phone—enticing you to come back here. But you've got to go, Leah. You need to go now, while he's inside."

"But then what?" Although she sounded slightly intrigued, she didn't budge.

He took his eyes off the door to look at her and, seeing the confused expression in her eyes, he knew the idea was half-hatched, but somehow he had to sell her on it. Just to get her to safety.

"I'm not really sure. But there's no time to waste. You need to run, Leah. *Now*."

"But I'm not sure about this plan." She frowned. "It sounds like a suicide mission...for you. And what does it accomplish?"

"It buys us some time. While you run as fast as you can into town—or to wherever you can get phone service—I'll be keeping your mom alive."

"How can you keep Mom alive if you're dead?" she asked stubbornly.

"You're our only hope. You've got to go now, Leah. Before Krantz comes back out. Call the state police again. If they refer you back to local law enforcement, call the FBI. And you'll have my phone with evidence, Leah. That should help convince someone we're not criminals."

"But I can't leave you behind. Krantz will kill you, Jon. You know he will."

"Not if I can convince him I'm worth more alive

than dead. That I'm his link to you. And if I was inside that building, maybe I'd think of something more to do. Maybe I could catch him off his guard, grab his gun…or something."

"Or get shot." She frowned. "That's what will probably happen."

"What if I could help your mom, Leah?"

She looked almost hopeful, then sadly shook her head. "It's too risky."

He pointed to his leg. "I didn't want to tell you this, but I'm not going to be able to run. I can barely walk."

"More reason I can't leave you here alone."

"Leah." He locked eyes with her. "This might be our only hope." He forced his phone into her hands. "You won't have connectivity for a while. That will buy me some time with Krantz. You're a fast runner, Leah. Without me to drag you down, you could make it—" Before he could finish, a sound from the compound made him turn to see that Krantz was emerging from the warehouse.

Jon considered standing up, holding his hands in the air and approaching. But he knew it was too dangerous to draw Krantz's attention over here. Chances were, he'd see Leah, too. And then it would be over for both of them. If only she'd listened to him—if only she'd taken off while she'd had the chance. Now it was too late.

Krantz gave the area one more long hard look, then unlocked the gate and, quickly relocking it, returned to his car and appeared to be using his radio. Jon wondered who he was contacting. Was he even still on duty? His civilian clothes seemed to suggest otherwise, but why did he still have the unmarked car? As Jon waited for Krantz to go, he wondered—how many other cops were crooked like Krantz? Was there anyone on the Cape Perpetua police force they could trust?

Eventually the sound of the car's engine signaled he was ready to leave and to Jon's relief, the dark car drove away. When it was well out of sight, he turned back to Leah. "It's not too late to make my plan work. You can still head for the jetty, get to a place where the phone connects and call for help."

"I hate to leave you here." Her eyes looked misty.

"At least you're not leaving me in Krantz's hands." He attempted a smile, feeling a bit of relief himself over this.

"That's true."

"And you're fast." He put a hand on her shoulder. "I'm guessing we could get help back here in a couple hours. Three at the most."

She looked at her watch. "That'd be around two."

He nodded.

"What if Krantz comes back before then?"

"I'll just lie low."

"But what if he decides to move my mom?"

Jon frowned. "Maybe that's when I go back to my earlier plan. I offer myself in exchange for your mom."

She looked tenderly at him. "Jon, I appreciate your valor—I really do—but I can't imagine it would work."

He shrugged. "Maybe not."

She looked up at the building. "I wish we could break into there."

He followed her gaze, cringing at the forbidding

razor wire. "Just getting over that fence would be a challenge. And those dead bolts look pretty tight."

"What about your Swiss Army knife and your survival upbringing?"

Jon tried not to grimace in pain as he slowly stood. "I could try to scale the fence. Maybe use the saw blade on my Swiss Army knife to cut that razor wire. Try to jimmy those locks."

"Or maybe I could," she suggested.

"No, this is a job for MacGyver." He made a weak smile.

"Let's walk around the compound," she suggested. "Find its weakest link."

"And let's hope no one's watching their security cam."

"Oh, yeah." She stopped in her tracks. "Maybe we should stay in the brush until we figure this out."

Keeping a safe distance and hiding in the shadows of the trees, they worked their way around to the back. The fence was tight and secure all the way around and with no back door or windows, the metal building was like a small fortress.

"You go around front," he told her. "Watch the road."

"What if you need my help?" She looked down at his bad leg with uncertainty.

"It'll be more helpful to have you warn me if Krantz returns." Jon pointed to what he felt certain was a security cam. "Once I start going up the fence, I'll probably be in plain sight. If Krantz is watching, he'll probably be right back."

"Okay. But if I see him what should I do? Yell?"

He considered this. "Can you make a hoot owl sound?"

She frowned. "I don't know."

"It sounds like this." He demonstrated a pretty authentic owl call, and she attempted to imitate him.

"Not bad."

"Be careful," she said gently.

He nodded. "You've got my phone. If anything goes wrong, it's back to plan A. Okay? You duck into the trees, then run toward the jetty."

She pursed her lips with a shadow of uncertainty in her eyes.

"Do you promise me, Leah?" He reached for her hand.

"I promise." She nodded solemnly.

Shaking her hand in agreement, he longed to just hold on to her, to lead her away from this ugly place— to run away together. But her mom was inside. They had to at least try to get her out.

After she was safely away, out of sight of the security cam, Jon stealthily approached the fence. He wasn't sure if he could do this with his bum leg, but there was no way he was going to let Leah attempt it. Chances were that Krantz was watching that camera right now. If he turned around and came back, he'd probably catch Jon red-handed. But at least Jon had made Leah promise. If anything went wrong, she was to run. He felt sure he could count on her.

Grasping the cyclone fence with his hands, he decided to just go for it. Despite the searing pain in his thigh, he clambered up to the top, careful to remain below the razor wire. Then, holding himself in place with his good leg, he got out his pocketknife, opened it to the saw blade and started to work on the wire. After he made a decent-size dent in it, he switched over to a small cutter tool and snapped it, causing it to spring out, catching him across his forearm and nearly making him lose his balance.

Silently praying, he carefully bent the nasty wire aside, making a small opening that he knew would be tricky at best to climb through. But somehow he made it over the top and was letting himself down onto the ground. With his heart pounding hard and his leg throbbing in pain, he went close to the building, hoping to be out of sight of the cameras, working his way around to the front of the building—and hoping that Leah was still keeping guard and that Krantz was nowhere nearby.

To his relief the front yard was still vacant with no sign of any vehicles on the road. Now he took out the wire he'd put in his pocket. Using it as well as his pocketknife blades, he attempted to jimmy the first dead bolt lock open. But it was not giving. He considered trying the other one, but knew that it would be useless, too.

He doubted that they could be opened from the inside, but decided to give it a try. Knowing that there could be someone in there guarding Leah's mom—and that this could be a bad move for him—he decided to go for it anyway. Pounding on the door, he called out. "Anyone in there? Can you unlock the door? Can you let me in? I've come to help!" He pounded again. "I've come to get you out of here!"

The voice of a girl responded. "We're in here!" she yelled. "Help us!"

"Can you open the door?" Jon yelled back.

"It's locked. We don't have a key."

"Who are you?" Jon yelled.

"Hallie Talbert," she yelled back.

"How old are you?" he yelled.

"Seventeen!"

"We're going to get you out of there," he shouted, looking over his shoulder to be sure no one was coming yet. "But don't tell anyone we've been here, Hallie. We'll get help as soon as we can. Just keep calm. *Okay?*"

"Okay."

"How is Mrs. Hampton doing?"

"The old woman?" Hallie called back.

"Yeah. Is she okay?"

"Yeah."

"Anyone else with you?" he yelled.

"Yeah. A girl from California. Her name is Rosita Garcia. She's only fifteen."

Jon felt even more sickened—and then enraged. "We want to help you, Hallie," he shouted.

"I heard him say that the boat is coming," Hallie yelled back.

"What boat?"

"To take us out of here."

"When?" Jon demanded.

"Tonight at high tide. They're taking us away." She let out a loud sob. "Please, help us!"

"We won't let them take you," Jon shouted.

"Please, please, help us!" She pounded on the door. "Please!"

"You need to stay calm," he told her again. "*And pray!* Ask God to help us!"

"I have been praying!" she cried.

"Good! And don't let on that we're here. *Keep calm.*" And now, worried that Krantz could be coming down the road, Jon limped back to the fence and, trying to block out the pain surging through his leg, he focused his energy on scaling the fence. But each step was excruciating. Finally, he reached the top, carefully slipping between the cut wires, trying not to fall.

He was barely over the edge when his bad leg slipped, giving him a hard landing on the other side. Doubling over in pain, he closed his eyes and took in a deep breath—begging for God to give him strength and a plan that would get those captives to safety.

"Are you okay?" Leah was beside him now, her hand laid gently on his back.

"We need to get out of sight," he huffed.

She wrapped a supportive arm around him, helping him to limp back into the surrounding brush behind the building.

"Let's stay in the shadows in case Krantz is on his way back." He leaned on her, wishing his leg were stronger as they made their way through the thick brush.

"The locks wouldn't give?" she asked.

"No. They were tight."

"Did I hear you talking to someone inside?"

He nodded, trying to catch his breath as he dragged his bum leg behind him.

"Did you talk to my mom?" she asked eagerly.

"No." He huffed. "But the girl said she's okay."

"What girl?"

"Hallie Talbert." He tried to get his breath. "She's seventeen. You need to remember that, Leah."

"Hallie Talbert, seventeen," she echoed.

"Another girl." He winced in pain as they pushed through a thick place of undergrowth. "Rosita Garcia. fifteen."

"Fifteen?" Leah sounded as shocked as he'd felt. "She's only fifteen?"

"Uh-huh. Memorize those names, Leah." He repeated them for her.

"Hallie Talbert, seventeen," she said. "Rosita Garcia, fifteen."

"When you call the state police—or FBI—you tell them those names. They must be aware that those girls have gone missing. It will help them to believe us this time."

"Okay." She sounded uncertain. "You still think I should go?"

"You've got to, Leah."

"But I hate to leave you—"

"You're their only hope. Our only hope. You have to make a run for it. There's no other way."

They'd made it all the way around to the other side of the building, to an overgrown area with a good view of the front of the compound.

"What about you?" she asked quietly. "What will you do?"

"I'll stay here and keep watch." He eased himself

onto a moss-covered fallen log, trying to catch his breath, trying not to show how much pain he was in.

"Will you remain out of sight?"

He turned to look directly into her eyes. "I might have to resort to plan A, Leah. If necessary, I'll reveal my whereabouts to Krantz."

"But he'll kill you."

"Not necessarily. And I'll only do it as my last resort. And just to buy us time—to prevent him from taking them away from here."

"Taking them away?" She frowned. "Where would he take them?"

Jon considered keeping this from her. He knew how worried she'd be for her mom if she knew she might be transported on a boat—to who knew where? And yet, he knew it was wrong to keep her in the dark. They were in this together. They had to be honest with each other. Besides, if something happened to him, she would need to know the details.

"Listen, Leah, Hallie told me something important just now."

"What?" Her eyes widened with concern.

"She must've overheard Krantz. It sounds like he plans to take them away from here. By boat tonight."

"By boat?"

"At high tide. I'm guessing they must run it up onto the beach. Pretty slick way to transport illegal drugs— apparently it works with people, too."

"Will he take my mom with them, too?"

"I don't know about that. But I'm sure the girls will be gone."

"We have to get them out of here, Jon."

"That's why you need to make a run for it, Leah. You have to get help. And if you can just make it to a place where the phone can connect—probably somewhere on the jetty." He dug his compass out of his pocket. "Take this for when you're in the trees. Just keep pressing south and you'll eventually run into the jetty. Hopefully the phone will work there. And you can send the video I shot to the state police. Or the FBI. Footage of a cop threatening to kill an innocent old woman—that alone should get their attention."

Leah pocketed the compass, then leaned over and, to his surprise, she wrapped her arms around him and held tightly to him. "I hate to leave you, Jon."

He returned the embrace, holding her close and wishing they had this moment under different circumstances. He'd been longing to take her into his arms. As he smelled the sweetness of her hair, the pain in his leg seemed to diminish. She felt so good next to him, as if she belonged there. As if they belonged together. "I hate to let you go," he said quietly. "But you have to, Leah."

She pulled away from him slightly, looking into his eyes with an intensity that nearly took his breath away. "If we never see each other again, Jon—if something happens to either of us and—well, I just want to tell you that I—"

"We *will* see each other again." He placed his hands on either side of her face, willing her to be strong—stronger than he was able just now. "You're going to get help, Leah. We're going to get out of this. And we're going to rescue your mom and those girls." And now, still holding her face, he pulled her gently toward himself and kissed her. He couldn't even believe that he'd done it—but just like that, as if it were meant to be, it had happened. And despite their hopeless situation, the kiss was sweet and promising and her eyes lit up as if she felt it, too.

"Okay." She smiled. "You're right. We will see each other again."

He reached into another pocket, extracting the half-full water bottle and the last energy bar. "Take these."

"No." She held up her hand. "You keep them."

"Take them," he insisted. "You need them more than I do."

"But I—"

"I mean it." He gave her his I-mean-business look and to his relief she didn't argue. "Now, run like the wind, darling."

"I will." She stood, holding up his phone. "See you in a few hours—hopefully with the state police, the FBI and the coast guard, too."

"Good for you!" He gave her his bravest smile, but as soon as she took off, he felt completely deflated with worry and fear. Sending her out like that—on her own and with Krantz well aware that they were in this vicinity. Well, it was just crazy. And he knew she'd have to run through some wide-open spaces to reach the jetty— the one place where everyone would expect the two of them to head for after they'd been spotted on the ATV going that way. What if Krantz was out there waiting for her right now? Perched on a high dune with his automatic rifle? She'd make an easy target.

ELEVEN

It was impossible to run through the wooded area. And in places, it was hard to simply walk. Thankful for Jon's compass, she kept it handy as she pushed through a particularly dense section of undergrowth. It would be so much easier to walk along the beach. But that would be too dangerous. She knew Krantz would be on the lookout for them today. And knowing that he had two kidnapped victims besides her mother made her even more aware of what a desperate man he was.

As she trudged along, she prayed. She prayed that God would lead her to someone who could help and that God would protect her mother and the two girls. And finally she prayed for God to keep Jon from harm. Her worst fear was that Krantz would return, and Jon would try to intervene with his plan A.

She understood Jon's thinking—that he might be able to buy them some time. And Jon, being an attorney, was probably good at reasoning with difficult people. But Krantz was not a rational man. He might just shoot Jon to get him out of the way. The thought of this sent a chill down her spine—and she prayed even harder for God to keep Jon safe. As she climbed over a fallen tree, she remembered the kiss. At first she'd been totally caught off guard by it. She suspected he had been, too. But after she'd recovered from the shock, she realized that it was the sweetest kiss she'd ever experienced. And she hoped it wouldn't be the last one.

Maybe she was wrong about Monica. Maybe when he'd told her it was over between them, he had meant it. Just because the woman was beautiful didn't mean that she was Jon's soul mate. For all Leah knew Monica could be a horrible person that Jon was fortunate to be rid of. Or she could be married to someone else by now. Hadn't Jon said it had been a year ago? A lot could happen in a year.

And what about how Jon had quizzed her about her own relationships? Why would he have been so curious to find out if she was single unless he was interested in her? And what about that kiss?

Please, God, don't let it be the last one!

Leah could hear the rumble of the ocean waves to her right and according to the compass, she was still going directly south. But according to her watch, she'd been walking for an hour. Shouldn't she have reached the jetty by now?

Seeing light coming through the trees up ahead, she knew she must be close. She also knew there was a dune area that ran alongside the jetty. A popular place for ATVs in the summertime or on a sunny weekend at other times of the year. But this was midweek and the off-season. The chances of someone being out here

today were slim. What she wouldn't give to run into a
friendly ATV enthusiast just now—someone to give
her a lift through this last stretch of dunes and over to
the road.

But when she reached the edge of the woods, leading
out to the open area of the dune, she met silence. She
looked all around, worried that Krantz could've staked
someone out here to watch for her. Or he might even
be here himself. She studied the tops of various dunes,
trying to determine if an irregularity was a clump of
grass or a tree or a sharpshooter hunkered down with a
high-powered rifle and scope pointed right at her. And
just because Krantz was a poor shot didn't mean that
his cohorts were, too.

Still hiding in the shadows of the wooded area, Leah
took out Jon's phone, hoping against hope that it might
be getting at least one bar here. Nothing. No connectivity whatsoever. Hopefully Jon was right about the
jetty. Hopefully she'd be able to use the phone there. If
nothing else, perhaps she could send a text. She could
explain the situation, tell them the location of the compound. And send the video, too.

In fact, she decided to start preparing a text. That
way she'd have it all ready to go as soon as she saw as
much as one bar of connectivity. Standing in the shadows, she carefully typed a message into the notepad.
She explained as best she could about the location of
the compound. Then she listed the names and ages of
the victims being held captive, as well as information
about Krantz and his plan to get the women out by boat
at high tide tonight. She also explained that Jon was an

attorney who'd been shot by Krantz and that she was a nursing student that Krantz had attempted to kidnap.

Feeling there was no more she could do and hoping that—if by chance—something should happen to her, the phone might still be useful for rescuing Jon and her mother and the girls—if it didn't fall into Krantz's dirty hands—she knew she needed to continue.

Breathing a silent prayer, Leah stepped out into the open area, bracing herself for the sounds of possible gunfire. But all she heard was the nearby surf and the screech of a gull. On high alert, she cautiously walked across the soft sand, watching all around her with each step. Although there were lots of tire tracks left from ATVs, there didn't appear to be any human footprints. She hoped that was a good sign.

Checking the compass, she spotted a twisted spruce tree that was due south and, knowing time was of the essence, she started to run toward it. The sooner she made it out of this cleared area, the better it would be. And once she reached the jetty, she would have a good solid surface to continue running. And hopefully phone connectivity.

She was only about a third of the way across the open dune when she heard the rumble of a helicopter coming from the direction of the jetty. Judging by the increasing whop-whop sound of the blades, it was headed her away. She stopped for a split second, trying to decide. Should she press forward or turn back?

If she pressed forward, she would have a long way to go before finding the shelter of trees. If she turned back, she might be able to get out of sight before the he-

licopter spotted her. And all her instincts said that was
why it was flying through this area. Whether it was the
coast guard or the police, they were probably searching
for the "dangerous criminals."

In that same split second, she decided on a third option. Instead of continuing forward to the jetty or retrac-
ing her steps, which would lead them back to where Jon
was camped at the compound, she turned east. Running
directly toward the preserve area, she wanted to make
them think she planned to cut across that really rugged
terrain. Even though it was full of swamps, quicksand
and black bears, she wanted them to believe she was
going that way in order to reach town.

But first she had to get out of this wide-open space.
Running as fast as she could through the soft, unstable
sand, she pressed toward the preserve. But each step felt
sluggish and slow and hard, just like a dream she used
to have as a child—running through a pool of Jell-O
with some villain chasing her. Only this was for real.

The sound of the helicopter blades was getting louder
and she knew it was over the dunes now. In Jon's mother's
purple warm-ups, she would be easy to spot out here. But
there was nothing to do but keep running—and to pray.

She glanced over her shoulder in time to see the helicopter diving down low—directly toward her. She was
disappointed to see it wasn't the bright orange coast
guard helicopter. If it were, she would've felt relatively
safe to surrender to them. Because she couldn't imagine
the coast guard would be in cahoots with Krantz. But
this was a small black helicopter and unless she was

mistaken, that was Krantz in the dark glasses, pointing down at her.

She heard the helicopter lifting up and circling back around, as if getting into a position. Were they going to land on the dune—and pursue her on foot? Or were they just getting better positioned to shoot her from up in the air? She didn't want to find out.

Arms and legs pumping as hard as she could make them go, she threw all of her energy into the last twenty feet of uphill sand between her and the trees. She could hear a man's voice yelling from the helicopter—probably Krantz, telling her to stop or he would shoot. But she was not stopping. If that was Krantz, it was too dangerous.

She had nearly reached the tree line when she heard the first shot. Making a zigzag trail, the way she'd seen in action movies, she continued without looking back. One more shot rang out, and now she was in the trees. But the strip along the dunes wasn't as overgrown as she'd hoped. Running from tree to tree, trying to stay in the shadows and out of sight, she pressed on into the denser brush ahead.

The helicopter was not giving up. And although her lungs were burning, she knew she needed to find a heavy thicket where she and her trail of footprints couldn't be spotted from the air. Fighting through the same kind of underbrush she'd just been so grateful to put behind her, and hearing the sound of the helicopter flying low overhead, she finally reached a thicket where the sky wasn't visible. Crouching down there, she paused to catch her breath. And taking a few gulps of water, she attempted to think and get her bearings. She looked at the compass, trying to calculate the best way to retrace her steps back to the compound and rejoin Jon.

The sound of the helicopter continued as it relentlessly circled in the sky above her. She could tell they were flying low, probably just above the treetops. And probably using their rifle scopes in the hope of spotting her—and shooting. But to her relief it also sounded as though they were expanding their search more to the east, deeper into the reserve and more toward town. It almost seemed that they'd fallen for her deception. She could only hope.

She continued to move through the woods, bearing her course northward and careful to stay in the densest thickets, which made moving tedious and slow, but it did allow her a chance to recover somewhat. Then, hearing the sound of the helicopter coming closer, she knew they were returning. Hopefully they didn't have some kind of a heat sensor that could pick her out from within the trees. She'd heard of things like that.

The helicopter circled around where she'd entered the preserve area a few more times and then finally sounded as if it was heading back toward the jetty. Feeling safe that she could run through a more open area, she took off, hoping to put more distance behind her as she worked her way back toward the compound. Pausing to check the compass, she realized that the helicopter engine was slowing down. It sounded as if it was landing in the nearby dune area.

She shuddered to think what might happen if it had

landed. Would they pursue her on foot? Imagining armed and determined men—led by Krantz—getting out in the dune area and following her trail across the sand, she knew she needed to move even faster now. It wouldn't be easy for them to track her through this area, but it wasn't impossible either. Not if they were good trackers. She just hoped they didn't have dogs with them. Then it would be hopeless.

Feeling exhausted and defeated, she trudged on, forcing one foot in front of the other. She checked her compass occasionally and even Jon's phone in the hopes she might pass through a hot spot. Straining her ears, she paused to listen, but all she could hear was the sound of the ocean. But that didn't mean they weren't following her on foot, although it wouldn't be easy out in this rough terrain.

At one point she looked around to see what she was actually trudging through and was startled to see water moving below the brush she was walking on. It looked like a stream or slough and it was at least six feet below her. She was actually walking high above the ground— that was how thick and tall the underbrush in these parts could grow. A coastal jungle. Seeing the water reminded her that she was thirsty.

She paused long enough to finish the last of the water from the bottle. She pushed on, wanting to find a place where she wasn't so high from the ground. What if she fell through? Would she ever be able to get out again? Finally, she came to a more open area with real ground beneath her feet. With treetops concealing her from the helicopter that she still heard passing by occasionally, she continued to walk, allowing herself to munch on the energy bar as she went. When she finished eating, she started to run again.

She had started cutting back toward the ocean in the hope that she'd find marks of the trail she'd made on her way to the jetty. Some broken branches or trampled-down brush. But it was useless. And she eventually discovered that she'd gone nearly to the beach. Wanting to remain somewhat under cover, she continued along the beach grass, working her way north on the edge of the dune. At least it was a little easier to travel that way. Where she was going? She wasn't even sure. Perhaps she'd end back up at the cabin.

But maybe the police would be gone from that area by now—out by the jetty or scouring the preserve area. And then she could climb the rock Jon had shown her and get phone connection up there—send the message she'd painstakingly prepared. As she ran, she vaguely wondered how many miles she would have gone by then. Certainly more than ten. Probably more like twelve. And much of that in rough terrain. If by some chance she got to run the Portland marathon in the summer, she should be in fairly good shape. Well, unless Krantz killed her.

As she slowed her pace to a fast jog, she could hardly believe that it had been less than twenty-four hours since her ordeal had begun. When would this madness end? And how would it end? Thoughts of reuniting with Jon helped to drive her as she continued moving north. But, worried that she'd overshot the compound area, she wondered if she'd ever see Jon again. And what if something had happened to him while she was gone? What if someone had come and taken her mom and the girls away while she was gone? What if Jon had been harmed trying to protect them? She couldn't allow herself to think about that.

She paused to look at her watch. According to her calculations she should've made it to the compound by now. Except for that side trip she'd taken to throw off her trackers. Who knew how far off that had taken her? She ventured beyond the beach grass now, looking over the top of the dune, down toward the beach, hoping for some familiar sign. The creek or some driftwood. But nothing along this stretch stood out particularly. Scanning the ocean, she noticed a boat out there. Probably a crabber. Unless it was a boat waiting to smuggle the kidnapped victims at high tide. That was possible.

Just before she turned back, she noticed a set of tire tracks on the beach. They appeared to have turned inland. Was that where they'd driven the ATV up the side of the dune? Although she saw no sign of its wreckage below. She continued jogging and as she got closer, she realized that the tire tracks seemed to lead to what looked like a beach access road. Not a road exactly, but it did look accessible. Maybe that was how Krantz had gotten his car down onto the beach to chase them this morning.

She hurried over to where the tire tracks cut through the dune, then followed them up until she realized they were merging into the same narrow rutted road that they'd followed to the compound earlier today. So she hadn't overshot the compound after all. Feeling strangely hopeful, she speeded up into a fast run.

And as crazy as it seemed, she felt as if she were almost home. Oh, it made no real sense. But somehow, the idea of being reunited with Jon—and knowing she was near her mother—appealed to her. Well, she thought, it was better than being out there by herself and being chased by a killer. She couldn't wait to see Jon again—hoping that he'd hold her in his arms as he'd done earlier. Well, after she'd foisted herself onto him.

Suddenly she felt defeated as the compound came into sight. Jon would be disappointed to find out she'd been unable to use the phone. She had failed at her mission. As she slowed down her pace, she realized that she was, quite literally, right back where she'd started. There was no help on the way. They were still in very serious danger. Perhaps even more so than before.

She approached the compound cautiously, remaining in the shadows in case someone besides Jon was around. But as she got closer, she could see there were no vehicles. That was a relief. But then, when she went to the place she'd left Jon, she didn't see any sign of him, either. Feeling a tightness in her chest that was more than just exhaustion, she went to their previous hiding spot. Not there, either. She walked all around the compound, quietly calling out to him, but he didn't answer. A chill went through her as she stood there. With his bad leg, he could barely walk. Where could he have gone?

She stared at the windowless brown building with its creepy security cams that resembled evil eyeballs. Was it possible that Jon had somehow done a MacGyver trick and gotten inside there? Or more likely, maybe Krantz or one of his cohorts had already been here and taken the hostages—as well as Jon? Perhaps they'd been monitoring those security cams and knew that she and Jon had been here. If that was the case, she would be a fool to stick around one minute longer than necessary.

She knew the only way to figure this out would be to scale that fence herself—to get inside and knock on the door in the hope that someone would answer. Even if Jon was gone, she could at least reassure herself that her mom was still here. Or not.

She had just reached the top of the fence and was about to go over when she heard the loud snap of a twig breaking behind her. She felt the hair on the back of her neck standing on end. Someone was watching her. Bracing herself for a gunshot, she knew she must decide. Jump over the fence and land in the compound area and use the building to hide behind? Or tumble back down on the outside of the fence and make a run for it? Neither option felt safe.

TWELVE

Leah was just about to release her hold on the fence and tumble backward when she heard Jon call out. "It's just me. Sorry to startle you."

"Jon!" she exclaimed as she eased herself back onto the ground. "You scared me." She turned to see him limping toward her with a look of pain in his face and something heavy in his arms. "I looked everywhere for you. Where've you been?"

"Rock hounding."

"What on earth for?" She hurried over and, seeing he was toting a rock about the size of a watermelon, she reached over to remove the bulky stone from his hold.

He looked relieved as he stood up straight. "Thanks. Sorry to be gone, but it took a while to find the right rock."

"What's it for?"

"I have a plan." He looked hopeful as he wiped the back of his hand over his moist brow. "Did you reach the state police or—"

"No." She glumly tipped her head over to where they'd hidden before. "Let's get under cover. Just in case they've tracked me."

"They?"

After they were tucked back into the brushy area, she explained about the helicopter, the rifle shots and trying to lead her pursuers into the preserve. "I wanted to throw them off, make them think I was trying to get to town."

"Was it a coast guard helicopter?"

"No." She described it to him.

"Sounds like a private copter. But that's reassuring. I'd like to believe the coast guard wouldn't cooperate with someone like Krantz, especially when he was attempting to shoot down an unarmed person."

"Me, too." She pointed to the large rock on the ground beside him. "Seriously, what is this for?"

"Plan B. Or maybe it's C or D. I think I've lost track." He made a tired sigh. "We know Krantz will be back here. If Hallie was right, and he plans to put them on a boat at high tide, which, according to this morning's tide, should probably be around seven or so this evening, I expect he'll show up around dusk. Maybe sooner."

"Yeah?"

He tapped the rock. "We'll wait for him to go inside the building and then I'll use this rock to break a side window and get into his car."

"Uh-huh?"

"I'll get his automatic rifle and when he comes out of the warehouse, I'll be ready for him. I'll catch him unawares and force him to drop his revolver, which I assume he'll have on him, or else I'll just shoot him."

Leah studied Jon. "You really think you can shoot him?"

"I *know* I can shoot him. I'm actually a pretty good marksman. I'm probably a better shot than Krantz, which isn't saying much." He made a half smile. "My grandpa was quite a hunter. He taught me to shoot when I was a kid."

"Okay." She nodded. "So you're a good shot. But do you really have the nerve to *kill* someone?" Leah wasn't sure that she could kill someone. Especially since her line of work was about saving and protecting life. And for some reason Jon did not strike her as a violent man. Maybe it was the kindness in his eyes.

"I didn't say I *would* kill him." He pursed his lips. "But I wouldn't mind incapacitating him—just enough to stop him and get him behind bars, where he belongs."

"Good."

"I'm hoping that once I get my hands on the rifle I'll have enough time to shoot that lock off the gate and get into the compound—I mean *before* Krantz comes out. That will give me a better chance of getting him before he figures out what's up."

"You'll have to move fast."

"I know."

"Maybe you should let me help," she said eagerly.

"No." He shook his head. "Too risky."

"But think about it, Jon. With your bad leg, you can't move that fast. Every second will be precious. If Krantz hears the rock crashing into his car, he could be out here in a flash."

"That's true."

"What if you're not ready for him?"

"It's a chance I'll have to take."

"Okay, what about a slight revision to your plan?" she asked hopefully.

"What kind of revision?" He looked doubtful.

"What if—as soon as Krantz goes inside—you get yourself positioned by the gate?" She pointed to the fence. "Meanwhile I could break in, grab the rifle and run it over to you—and you'd be all set to shoot open that lock. It'd be lots faster."

"I don't know, Leah. That rock is heavy. Do you think you could even hoist it through a car window?"

She stood now, picking up the rock. "Watch, I'll show you." Then, pretending Krantz's car was parked where he'd parked it earlier today, she held the rock over her head and, using both hands, she threw it sideways like it was going through a side window. To further make her point, she pretended to reach through the invisible window and open the door, then she grabbed the pretend gun and sprinted to the gate. All within a few seconds, too.

"Impressive." Jon clapped quietly as she picked up the rock and after roughing her running shoe through the dent the rock made in the sand, as well as scuffing over her footprints, she hurried back to join him, dropping the rock with a dull thud.

"I'd venture to say that if we both went through the same little exercise—and timed it—I would be the winner."

He arched one brow. "Are you always this competitive?"

"Just when it comes to life and death." She made a sheepish smile. "Okay, maybe I'm competitive at other times, too. But I'm not a sore loser…not usually anyway."

"For someone so small, you're pretty strong." He reached over to test her biceps muscle, which she flexed with pride. "You must do weights or something."

"Working in the nursing home, we have to lift and move our patients a lot. It helps to be in good shape."

He leaned back into the log with a weary sigh. "Normally, I'm not such a wimp, but this leg is killing me."

She nodded sympathetically. "I think that wound was worse than I thought. And all that running probably tore into some muscle. I can't imagine how painful that must be. When we get out of this mess, you'll probably require some surgery to get it put back together right."

"When we get out of this mess…"

She looked at her watch. "If Krantz doesn't come until dusk, we could have a couple of hours to gather our strength." She turned to him. "Take a nap if you want, I can keep watch."

"I don't think I can sleep." He frowned over at the building. "And maybe, just to be safe, we should go over my plan again."

"You want me to go do my demonstration again?" she said in a teasing tone.

"No, that's not necessary. But let's work out the details, starting with right after you hand me the rifle, okay?"

"Good idea."

"So as soon as I've got the rifle, I want you to take off for the other side. You know the spot where we hid the first time we came here?"

"Yeah." She nodded.

"I will have shot the lock open and will go inside, hopefully before he comes out. I'd like to be right next to the door so that I can really take him by surprise."

"But what if you can't get there before he comes out?"

"Then I'll just have to take him by surprise however I can."

"What about staying behind his car?" she suggested. "Then you could use it as a shield."

He seemed to consider this. "I suppose if I didn't make it clear to the door, that might be a good backup plan. But I really hope this won't be a shoot-out."

"What if he brings them out with him?" she asked suddenly. "I mean, like, he could use my mom or a girl as a human shield. What then?"

"That's why I wanted to be all the way in the compound. So that I could come at him from the side, instead of head-on. It seems the safest way to shoot him without hurting anyone else. If he refuses to drop his revolver."

"What if he takes his rifle inside with him?"

Jon frowned. "I really don't see why he'd do that. He'll need his hands somewhat free if he's going to get his hostages out and into the car."

"You're probably right."

"So mostly we just really need to break into his car as quietly as possible, Leah."

"Is that possible?"

He glumly shook his head. "Probably not."

"So, really, we just need to be as fast as we can."

"Yeah."

"I have an idea." She stood up. "What if I tip off the girls and my mom—inside the compound. I'll let them know we're trying to rescue them and if there's a way they can slow things down inside—stall somehow—that it might help us to do this."

He slowly nodded. "Not a bad idea."

"I'll be right—"

He grabbed her hand. "But I don't like you being in the compound, Leah. Too dangerous."

"I'll be really quick," she promised. "You can keep a lookout on the road. You see anything and you can just signal. Do your hoot owl call. And I'll hotfoot out of there and I'll come back around through the brush." She looked at her watch. "Come on, Jon, the sooner I do this, the better."

"Okay." He looked uneasy as he pushed himself to his feet. "I'll watch the road. Just keep your ears peeled."

"Done." And now she sprinted around to the back, but before she climbed the fence, she removed the loose warm-ups, tossing them on the ground. Too much fabric with too much potential to get snagged up on those nasty barbs. She quickly scaled the fence again, gingerly slipping between the cut razor wire, then turning around to let herself down into the yard. She paused for a split second, listening to the still air around her. No owls.

She dashed around to the front of the building, glancing over to where Jon was still positioned by the road before she started beating on the door. "I'm here to help you," she yelled. "Hallie? Rosita? *Mom?*" Then she called out her mom's name. "*Ellen*, are you still in there? *Hello?* Can anyone hear me?"

"We're here," a girl's voice answered. "Who are you?"

"I'm Leah. I think my mom's in there. Is Ellen still there?"

"Yeah. Can you let us out? *Please?*"

"Are you Hallie?" Leah asked.

"Yes. I'm Hallie. *Please, get us out of here—please!*"

"We're working on a plan." Leah looked over her shoulder to make sure Jon was still watching the road. "But we need your help, Hallie. When Krantz—the creep who kidnapped you—gets back inside there with you guys, I need you to do something to stall him a little while."

"What?"

"We need you to stall him. Make a fuss or something. Just slow him down, okay?"

"Okay."

"It sounds like he plans to transport you all by boat. But you need to do something to waste some time so that we can rescue you. Okay?"

"Okay! Just get us out of here. Please!"

"You help us, Hallie. So that we can help you. Do you understand?"

"Yeah! *Stall Krantz.*"

"That's right."

"And you'll get us out of here?"

"Yes!" Leah checked on Jon. "Is Ellen okay?"

"She's been crying all day. But she's asleep now."

"Good. She's got some memory problems, and she

gets confused," Leah explained. "Please, help her if you can."

"I will. But please get us out of here," Hallie pleaded again.

"We plan on it! It won't be long now." As Leah ran around the back of the compound, she heard three distinct hoots. Jon was warning her! Krantz was on his way! With a pounding heart, she grabbed onto the fence, hurrying to reach the top and trying to be silent. But on the top, she nearly slipped as she was trying to turn around and maneuver past the razor wire. A scream froze in her throat as she grabbed onto the chain-link fence, clinging tightly as she dangled over the edge.

Instead of climbing down, she simply dropped to the ground. As she grabbed the discarded warm-ups, she heard another set of hoots and wasn't sure which way to go. If Krantz was in front, she didn't want to blast around the other side. But she didn't want to get stuck back here, either. So she raced for the brush, leaping right into it in order to hide herself and get her bearings.

Krantz had to be here to pick up the girls—and her mom, too! That meant she needed to get around to the front of the compound, to rejoin Jon—ASAP—or else their plan for breaking into the car would be ruined. As she stealthily worked her way through the bushy undergrowth, she tried to listen for the sound of an approaching car, but all she could hear was the rustling of the brush as its sharp thorns tore into her bare legs.

When she reached the side of the building, she paused, straining her ears, trying to listen for the sound of a car engine or Krantz's footsteps—or even Jon's hoot owl warning. But not hearing a single sound—not even the birds—she was afraid to move. Was it possible that Krantz had shown up on foot? What if he had other trackers with him? The ones who'd been with him in the helicopter, dropped off in the dunes. What if they already had Jon in custody? He would be defenseless against a group of armed men. A nearby rustling sound sent a chill through her. Holding her breath, she waited. Was that them? Were they here? What now?

THIRTEEN

Still frozen in place and barely able to breathe, Leah tried to decide her best course of action. Retreat farther into the woods? Attempt a hoot owl sound and see if Jon answered? She'd heard nothing that sounded like a car. No tires crunching, no engine noise, no car door closing. No car meant no rifle to steal. And no need to risk exposing herself by returning to Jon to assist with the rock throwing. But what should she do? Stay here? Move quietly toward the front of the building? *What?*

She heard the rustling sound again, followed by Jon's voice. *"False alarm."* He was calling out to her from the front of the building.

Seriously? Still clutching the warm-ups to her chest, she slowly stood, looking all around her before she cautiously made her way back to where she'd left him. As much as she felt relieved, she also felt the pain of the fresh scratches incurred by leaping into the nasty underbrush. "What's going on?" she asked as she rejoined him.

"Sorry about the false alarm." He was still squinting

down the road. "I really thought I heard a car engine, thought it was coming this way. I jumped the gun. But let's get out of sight just in case."

"Well, I guess it's better to be safe than sorry." She slipped her arm around his waist, helping him to walk back to their most recent hiding spot.

"Thanks." He clung to her shoulders, leaning into her.

"I nearly fell off the top of the fence when I heard your hoot owl noise." She attempted a chuckle. "I was so scared."

"Sorry about that." He peered curiously at her when they reached their hiding spot. "Hey, what happened to your clothes?"

"I pulled a Peter Rabbit," she said wryly.

"Huh?" He eased himself down to the ground, leaning against the fallen log with a tired sigh.

"Didn't your mom ever read you that story as a child?" She tugged the velour pants on over her running shorts, noticing how grubby and torn they'd gotten. But at least they'd offered some protection to her legs. Not that they'd last much longer.

"Maybe. I don't recall."

"Peter loses his clothes when he sneaks under the garden gate to get away from Mr. McGregor." She pulled on the jacket, zipping it up and patting the zipped pocket to be sure Jon's phone was still there. She removed it, showing it to him. "The battery is about half now. We better power down."

"For sure."

She turned it off, then held the phone out to him.

"You keep it, Leah. While I'm driving us out of here, you can be trying to get a signal—and call for help."

She frowned at his bad leg. "You sure you can drive with that wound?"

He nodded. "Positive."

She zipped the phone back into her pocket, removing the crumpled plastic water bottle from her other pocket. "I wanted to find a place to refill this," she said, "but I—"

"Listen." Jon held a forefinger to his lips.

She froze, straining her ears to hear. "I think that's a boat on the ocean," she finally whispered. "I know it sounds closer, but sound travels over water."

He nodded. "I think you're right. Listen, it's gunning its engine. So I did hear something. Just not a car."

"And I noticed a boat a couple miles out on my way back here," she explained. "Looked like a crabber, but maybe it's the one that's supposed to pick up the girls tonight."

"Makes sense they'd use something that looks like a fishing boat or crabber. Easier to overlook." He frowned. "I sure hope this is the night and that Krantz is the one coming back here."

"You think it could be someone else?"

"It stands to reason that there are some other creeps involved in this."

"Well, even if it's a different car—are we still breaking into it?" she asked.

"What choice do we have?"

"But what if there's no gun inside the car?"

"A chance we have to take. If there's no gun and the keys are inside, we'll just steal the car."

"And leave Mom and the girls behind?" She looked at him in alarm.

"How else will we get help?"

"You're right." She slowly nodded. "I just hope it's Krantz's car—with his gun inside."

"Me, too. I really want to get my hands on that rifle—and on him."

"So let's say that it is Krantz—what's the rest of the plan? What will we do with him once you get him to surrender his revolver?" Even as she said this, she wondered if that would even happen. Krantz was stubborn and mean. He might rather go down shooting than surrender. What if he killed Jon first?

"I have most of the logistics figured out." He rubbed his chin. "After I secure his gun, we'll get him on the ground and you'll help me tie him up. Hopefully we can find some rope or something inside the warehouse that will work."

"Right. Then what?"

"I'll get his keys. We'll leave him here, securely locked in the warehouse." He made a mischievous grin. "Give him a taste of his own medicine. And then we'll drive the girls and your mom out of here. Hopefully we can make it to town without being recognized. And with Krantz tied up like that, he won't be able to alert anyone about what happened. As soon as we get to a place with connectivity, you'll start calling the state police or coast guard or FBI. And then we'll just keep driving until we reach someplace safe." He frowned. "Maybe the coast guard station. Or the fire station in town. Or maybe just a restaurant where there are other people around."

"A restaurant." She sighed. "Food…"

He grimaced. "Yeah, I'm starving, too."

She frowned. "I hope Ralph is okay."

"I'm sure he's fine. Probably snoozing comfortably, dreaming about chasing rabbits."

She looked into his eyes. "Do you think we'll really make it out of here tonight, Jon? In Krantz's car? With my mom and the girls? You think we'll really get free?" As she asked him this, she felt a lump growing in her throat. Maybe it was just plain exhaustion and hunger and fear, but she was feeling totally hopeless and on the verge of tears. She wouldn't admit it, but Jon's desperate plan sounded worse than impossible to her. So many things could go wrong.

"We have to get out of here," he said solemnly.

"Yeah." She glanced at her watch. "So I guess he could be here in an hour or two," she said quietly. "Until it's dark and the tide comes in."

"We should probably try to get some rest until then… help us be prepared for what's ahead."

She leaned against the log next to him, trying not to imagine what felt like a suicide mission. "Feel free to snooze if you want. I'll stay awake. I'll just nudge you if I hear the car—or anything else." She still wasn't convinced the search party wouldn't show up on foot—or with dogs. What she and Jon would do if that happened—she had no idea. She glanced at Jon, curious as to whether he was having any of the same doubtful thoughts as she was. But he actually looked somewhat at ease.

"I don't think I could sleep," he said quietly. "But it does feel good to relax."

"Yeah. I can't remember ever feeling as sore and tired as I do right now. A marathon sounds easier."

"You've done a lot of running under some pretty horrific circumstances. I'm impressed you can still walk."

"I was thinking the same about you—and with your gunshot wound. That's impressive, too."

"Well, I was kind of surprised that I could carry that rock back here. It wasn't exactly nearby." He made a lopsided grin. "But I'm not as tough as you."

She wrinkled her nose. "I'm guessing you're a lot tougher, Jon. Under normal circumstances anyway."

"Normal circumstances..." He shook his head. "It's hard to remember what normal feels like."

"I know." As she gazed into his dark brown eyes, she wished these were "normal circumstances." She wondered how they would behave if they were. Or had they simply been forced into a relationship that would never have evolved in the real world? And yet she knew they'd both felt some chemistry. She hadn't imagined that.

Remembering the kiss they'd shared sent a warm flush up her neck and into her cheeks. Certainly *that* wasn't just a fluke, was it? Did people normally kiss when feeling fearful for their lives? Was it possible to fall in love under *abnormal* circumstances? Or was romance limited to normal? Leah wasn't sure.

But she was sure about this—she and Jon lived in totally different worlds. Jon and his parents were well-educated attorneys. And from what she had seen— based on their lovely vacation cabin and their ocean cruise—this family was pretty well-off, if not down-right wealthy. Meanwhile, Leah was barely scraping by. With her mom in nursing home care, she had spent the past few years working two part-time jobs just to support herself and pay for nursing school. She was a scrapper trying to carve a future for herself. And yet Jon was reconsidering his law career in order to pursue art—taking time off just to figure things out. Their lives were as different as night and day.

"What are you thinking about?" he asked with quiet curiosity.

"I don't know." She shrugged and looked away.

"You seemed pretty deep in thought."

Feeling trapped, she tried to come up with something else. Something not quite so revealing. But something that might foster an open discussion—related to the kiss. Because, really, it was that kiss that had got her going down these mental rabbit trails. "Earlier today, when I was out there running for my life trying to get phone connectivity, I actually had some time to think." She looked back at him now. "And I realized how devastated I'd be if I didn't see you again, Jon. I mean, if anything happened to you—I would be really sad."

His eyes seemed to warm. "I was having similar thoughts, Leah. I was really worried that you might get caught on your way into town. That was pretty disturbing. Consequently, I was praying really hard for your safety." He smiled. "I'm glad you made it back in one piece."

"Thanks. I was praying for you, too."

"But I have kind of a strange confession to make." He

seemed troubled. "I was actually worried about you finding safety. Like, what would happen if you made it all the way to town with no problem? That concerned me."

"You're kidding. *Why?*"

"Because that would end our time together." He shook his head with a funny expression. "I know that sounds completely nuts. And I suppose I'm not totally serious—I mean, I *do* want us to make it out of this. But a part of me didn't want it to end." He made a sheepish smile. "Because I've really enjoyed getting acquainted with you, Leah."

"Me, too." She smiled sadly as the realization hit her. He was confirming her doubts. Justifying her concerns that their meeting was a fluke. Here she'd been longing for *different* circumstances when the problem was that they were from *different* worlds. Their precarious relationship would naturally dissolve once they were out of this mess. End of story. And, really, she told herself— getting out of this mess and back to her previous life should be enough. If they made it out alive, she should be nothing but hugely grateful.

Despite his claim at being unable to sleep, Jon closed his eyes and, judging by his even breathing, he was either asleep or deeply resting. Not wanting to disturb him with more conversation, Leah simply studied his profile. There was no denying Jon Wilson was a very handsome man. Perhaps even more so when he wasn't aware that he was being stared at. She was tempted to use his phone to take a photo of him. Something she could later send to herself—when they were safe. Something she could keep to remember him by—after this relationship ended. Because deep inside her, she knew they would part ways. Oh, he'd be polite about it. Maybe he'd even promise to call sometime. But he wouldn't. Guys like Jon just didn't fall for girls like Leah. Not in her experience anyway.

She suddenly remembered that amazing painting of Monica. Now, that was the kind of girl that someone like Jon Wilson fell for. Beautiful, sophisticated, probably well educated and probably from a wealthy family of influence. Of course, this reminded her that she'd never really heard the rest of the Monica story. Even though she'd tried to get him to open up, Jon had seemed somewhat evasive. Almost as if that story wasn't over yet. Oh, he'd acted as if there was nothing to talk about, but she'd still felt uncertain. Not to mention insecure.

Leah knew that this particular brand of insecurity— feeling inferior to a woman like Monica—was her own personal problem. Something she'd learned in middle school because of mean girls—and something she'd been determined to have gotten over by now. She hated to admit to this to anyone, even herself, but she had never been comfortable around "beautiful" women. She sometimes told herself she didn't have time for those impeccably dressed, picture-perfect women—the ones with perfectly manicured nails and every hair in place. But the truth was they made her nervous. Oh, she admired them sometimes from a safe distance, but she did not relate to them. Not at all.

Leah had always been a hands-on, can-do, roll-up-your-sleeves kind of girl. No time for hair and nails and makeup. Proud to be a tomboy. More interested in sports than fashions and fads. This was partly from not having had a dad in the home, and partly because her mother had never been a particularly strong person. Even as a child, Leah had been the one to pick up the slack—wherever her mother happened to drop it, which she'd done a lot. More so as she'd gotten older.

The fact was that Leah prided herself on being independent and strong. And she felt fairly certain she could never relate to someone like Monica, much less be her friend. In Leah's eyes, which were probably judgmental and possibly inaccurate, Monica seemed like an entitled princess. The kind of girl who was used to getting what she wanted. And, unless Leah had misread the expression in the eyes of the sketches and painting, Monica had wanted Jon.

Also, it bothered her that someone as seemingly "down-to-earth" as Jon had been involved with a girl like Monica, who seemed the princess type. It just didn't make sense. Of course, now she had to question whether she really knew Jon as well as she presumed. She resisted the urge to reach over and push a strand of hair off his forehead—too personal.

She reminded herself—harshly—that they had only been acquainted since yesterday. *Twenty-four hours?* Was it possible? Was that all the time that had passed since their first encounter with Krantz? Leah frowned at her watch. It felt like days. Maybe even a week. And she felt as if she hadn't eaten or slept for a week. She looked up into the sky to see that it was starting to get dusky. The sun must've gone down a few minutes ago. It wouldn't be too long until high tide now.

She turned back to Jon, relieved to see that he seemed to be soundly sleeping. As a nurse, she knew how restorative sleep could be for a patient's recovery. It wouldn't repair his leg, but it might help him to get through the next couple of hours. Because no matter what happened, the rest of their night was not going to be easy.

Jon suddenly opened his eyes, making her turn away from staring at him. "You okay?" he asked quietly.

"Yeah...sure," she answered. "Just thinking."

"I guess I dozed off."

"I'm sure you needed it."

"What were you thinking about?" he asked in earnest. "You looked pretty serious."

She sighed, wishing she could be totally honest about all the thoughts that had just been tumbling through her head. Wishing she had the nerve to question him about his feelings toward Monica. Wishing she could ask him the meaning behind their shared kiss earlier. But maybe she wasn't any more ready for that than he was. Apart from feeling intrusive, she wasn't sure she wanted to hear his truthful answer in regard to the lovely Monica. Besides, she chided herself—this wasn't the time or the place for this conversation. Perhaps there would never be a proper time or place.

So, eager for a distraction, she brought up the dog. "I wonder how Ralph's doing right now."

"You left water and food, didn't you?"

"Yeah." She frowned. "I just hope he's not feeling lonely."

Jon made a half smile. "Don't worry, he'll be all

right. Now that Krantz knows we're out here somewhere, he won't be focusing on the house."

She turned her attention to the warehouse building now. "I wonder how this place ever got built. I can't imagine it was permitted way out here."

"Not with the protected dunes and the preserve area."

"As far as I know, building isn't allowed in these parts. Residential or commercial." She sighed. "Probably why some people warned me it wasn't safe to run out on this stretch of beach. Too deserted."

"This place obviously went up under the radar. My guess is that Krantz and his buddies hauled materials in here at night." He narrowed his eyes as he studied the ugly building. "Pretty shoddy construction, too. Those metal sheets don't even look properly screwed down." He suddenly sat up, then turned to her. "Hey, I think I could get under one of the metal sheets. Just remove a few screws, then bend the metal up. We might be able to slip the hostages out through the side."

"Do you have the right tools on your Swiss Army knife?" she asked hopefully.

"I might." He was just reaching into his pocket when she heard something.

"Wait." She put a hand on his arm, nodding toward the road. "I don't think that's a boat."

"Sounds like a car coming," he whispered.

Hunkering down behind the brush in the dusky damp air, they both waited and listened as the sound of a motor drew closer. It was definitely not a boat.

Leah felt her legs trembling as the sound of the car grew closer, and seeing the bright headlights through the brush sent a chill down her spine. This was it—time to pull off Jon's big plan. She prayed that it would work as they hoped. Prayed that she'd have the strength to smash the car window with Jon's rock. Prayed that they'd free the hostages and escape to safety.

As the car passed right in front of them and the headlights swept the brush, every muscle in her body grew tense. The car then turned around to face out to the road, backing up close to the gate. She felt a mixture of relief and disgust to see that it was Krantz's unmarked car. The same dark vehicle that had pulled her over yesterday. She couldn't see through the tinted windows, but she felt certain Krantz was behind the wheel.

This was it! Their chance to catch him in his own nasty trap, to turn him in to the authorities, to make him pay the price for his criminal ways. Everything in her felt ready now. Like a tightly wound spring, she was primed to jump into action. Just as soon as Krantz was safely inside the warehouse, she would pick up the rock and race over to the car.

As the car engine was turned off, Leah turned to Jon, giving him what she hoped looked like a self-assured nod—to indicate they could do this thing. He nodded back, and she felt a surge of confidence rush through her. Together they would take this thug down. They would rescue her mother and the girls—and get them safely out of this dark, horrible place. It was about to really happen!

Waiting for Krantz to emerge from the car, Leah replayed her role in Jon's plan. She glanced at the stone sitting right next to her, imagining how she would jump to her feet, pick it up and dash to the driver's side of the car. Jon had suggested that side was best for grabbing the rifle out of its holder between the front seats. She'd hoist the rock high, aiming it dead-center of the side window and then, using her full force, she would slam it down. She was just imagining reaching into the car when she heard the car door opening.

Holding her breath, she waited—watching as Krantz emerged from the car. He was still dressed in dark clothes, but the sunglasses were gone, exposing narrowed eyes that were cautiously darting all about—almost as if he knew he was being watched in the dusky light. And then to her horrified surprise, the passenger door opened from the other side. Another man, shorter and smaller than Krantz, got out. With a black stocking cap pulled low on his brow, he, too, was dressed in dark clothing.

Leah exchanged a frightened glance with Jon and knew they were both thinking the same thing—this was not part of the plan. It seemed unlikely for Jon, with his wounded leg, to catch Krantz by surprise and get him down to the ground—but a second man? That sounded impossible. And extremely dangerous. Maybe it was time to abort the mission. Come up with a different plan. But what?

"We need to get moving." Krantz fumbled with a ring of keys. "Mack's bringing the dory in right now. He expects us to meet him by six-thirty."

"Want me to wait out here?" Stocking Cap asked in a gruff voice.

"Nah. I need you to help me get them out of there.

Three of 'em are a handful. And that Hallie might look like an angel, but she's a wildcat. You grab her—and make sure you get her hands cuffed good and tight before you bring her out. I'll take care of the other two."

"Got it."

Krantz got the gate open, but from what Leah could see, he didn't bother to lock it behind him. That was one thing in their favor. But two guys? That really changed the odds of this working. She glanced back at Jon again, ready to throw in the towel, but his eyes looked determined. As soon as Krantz and his buddy were inside the building, he was on his feet. "Let's do this," he said quietly but firmly.

"But there are two—"

"I know, Leah. It's our only chance. Bust open that window and run that gun to me. I'm going in now. Be fast!" he hissed.

"Okay…" She picked up the rock and, without saying another word, they both started to move toward the compound. Within seconds she was beside the car with both hands hoisting the rock above her head. Praying for the strength of Samson, she slammed the rock into the side window and watched as the shatterproof glass crumbled into neat tiny squares beneath the weight. But the sound of the breaking glass was loud. The men had to have heard it inside.

With a pounding heart, she hurried to open the door. Feeling certain that Krantz had to be outside by now, probably aiming his revolver right at her head, she reached for the automatic rifle, drew it out and turned.

FOURTEEN

Stunned to see the warehouse door still closed, Leah sprinted over to where Jon was waiting. He looked somewhat surprised, too, but as she got closer to the building she heard the sounds of people shouting and screaming inside. This had to be Hallie's attempt to stall Krantz. *Good girl!*

"Run!" Jon commanded as he grabbed the gun.

Without a word, Leah ran to the area where Jon had told her to wait. By the time she got there, Jon had his back against the building. The gun was aimed toward the door, and Jon looked ready to shoot. Even though the dusky light was getting dimmer she could still see the determined look on his face. Although he looked tense and ready, she knew this wasn't going to be easy. Anything could go wrong. And two men! How would Jon manage?

She tried to envision how it would go down when Krantz and his buddy eventually emerged. Would they have the girls and her mother in front of them? All coming out at once? And, if so, how would Jon make the men take him seriously without risking the others? Praying in urgent silence, Leah thanked God for the distraction tactics that had gone on inside and pleaded for God to continue helping them, begging Him to keep her mom and the girls safe—and to bring those horrid men to justice.

Jon waited by the building, and he suddenly seemed so vulnerable. Barely able to walk and worn-out. What if he couldn't get a clear shot at the men? Or if the cowards used their victims as human shields? One shot was all it would take—from either Krantz or his cohort—and Jon would be gone. She prayed even harder for God to protect him. *Keep him out of the line of fire.*

Just then, the door burst open. The light from inside made the figures look like shadows to Leah, but Jon must've seen them better because he burst into action.

"Drop to your knees!" he shouted.

By now Leah could see that Krantz had Rosita and her mom, but, surprised by Jon, he immediately released them. In the same instant that Rosita tugged Leah's mom back inside the building, Krantz went for his revolver—and Jon shot. Leah watched in stunned relief as Krantz crumbled to the ground. Yelling in pain, he dropped his gun into the shadows.

"Freeze!" Jon yelled at the other man, holding the rifle on him as the three females cowered inside the door.

Before Jon could say another word, she sprinted toward them. She knew that the revolver was still within Krantz's reach, and he was going for it. But Jon needed to keep his attention on the other guy. Plus, with his bum leg, he wouldn't be able to leap for the gun. Not the way she could.

"Let the girl go!" Jon yelled at Stocking Cap. "Get on your knees!" Meanwhile Krantz continued writhing on the ground, moaning in pain as he inched closer to his gun.

"No!" Leah screamed as she stomped hard on Krantz's outstretched hand, stopping him from getting his revolver. He swore as he jerked back his injured hand, glaring at her with dark, beady eyes. She kicked the gun away from him, but before she could snatch it up, someone jumped her from behind. Grabbing her ponytail, Stocking Cap wrapped his other arm tightly around her neck as he dragged her toward the gate. Keeping her in front of him for a shield. And now the girls and her mother began screaming and crying.

"Put her down or I'll shoot," Jon yelled.

"No, you won't!" Stocking Cap taunted.

Leah knew Jon couldn't possibly get a clean shot. And the revolver was still on the ground. She suddenly remembered her high school self-defense class. Pulling an elbow high, she came down with a fast, solid blow directly into Stocking Cap's rib cage. He gasped in pain, loosening his grip on her. In the same instant, she spun around, delivering a hard kick. Stocking Cap doubled over and, cursing in pain, he took off through the gate. Jon shot twice, but Stocking Cap kept running, escaping into the dark wooded area.

"Let him run," Jon yelled at Leah. His rifle was still aimed at Krantz. "Come help me with this lowlife."

Leah dashed back over. "Sorry," she said as she scooped up the revolver. "But I saw Krantz going for—"

"It's okay. You did the right thing. And Krantz's little buddy was unarmed. I expect that's the last we'll see of him." He glanced at Leah, but she knew this wasn't over yet.

Jon fished his pocketknife out and handed it to her. "Go find something to tie Krantz up with," he instructed. "I'll keep watch out here."

Still holding the revolver, Leah went into where the girls and her mom were still cowering in the doorway. Their hands were bound with nylon handcuffs. She paused to hug her mom. "It's going to be okay." Not surprisingly, her mom didn't register any recognition. In times of high stress—like this—her Alzheimer's was always at its worst. Leah turned to the tall blonde girl that had to be Hallie.

"You did a great job tonight, Hallie." Leah used the knife to cut the handcuffs off the teen. "Can you free Rosita and my mom now?" She handed her the knife. "While I find something to tie up Krantz."

"Yeah." Hallie took the knife. "There's a box of rope and junk in the kitchen."

"Kitchen?" Leah looked around the creepy building.

"That table over there," Hallie explained. "We call it the kitchen."

Leah picked her way through piles of trash and crates and bottles and miscellaneous junk. The place reeked of human filth—of people in captivity without access to plumbing. Leah cringed as she saw the kitchen. Unwashed moldy cans of partially eaten beans and other things overflowed from a cardboard box on the floor. A bucket of grungy-looking water with a tin cup was next to it. Drinking water? She was not that thirsty.

She rummaged around until she found a plastic box that did have some rope in it. Grabbing a coiled bundle of nylon cord, she hurried to the door, picking up a T-shirt from the floor as she went. It was dirty, but it would work as a bandage for Krantz's leg. He might get an infection, but at least he wouldn't bleed to death.

"Hallie," she called out, seeing the girl had gotten the handcuffs off the others. "Can you help me get this man tied up and back in here? My friend Jon has a bad leg, and we need to move fast."

"Yeah." Hallie followed her out and, seeing Krantz still on the ground, she gave him a solid kick in the back.

"Easy does it," Leah said gently to Hallie. "He'll get what's coming to him."

"He'd better."

Leah and Hallie rolled Krantz over on his stomach, tying his hands tightly behind his back before they rolled him back over. Already he had a good puddle of blood in the sandy dirt. Leah took a moment to examine the gunshot wound to his leg. Unlike Jon's wound, this one had gone right through the center and, Leah suspected, had shattered the bone. Krantz wouldn't be walking anytime soon.

Leah wrapped the T-shirt snugly around his thigh, bandaging it as tightly as she could without making it a tourniquet, which wasn't necessary.

"Why are you helping *him*?" Hallie demanded angrily. "He's a monster!"

"I know. But I don't want him to bleed to death while we're gone," Leah said as she tied it off.

"Why not?" Hallie scowled. "He deserves to die."

"Maybe, but I'd rather see him go to prison." Leah reached for the nylon cord.

"We'll get him inside," Leah told Jon. She paused to instruct Hallie on how to lift him, then they dragged him back into the warehouse, dumping him on the floor next to the table in the "kitchen."

"I've got his keys," Jon called out. "Send your mom and the other girl out to the car. Then hurry!"

"Tie his feet together," Leah told Hallie. "Then we'll secure him to the table."

While Hallie was hog-tying Krantz, Leah went to Rosita. "I know you're scared, honey," she said gently. "But help Ellen, okay? She's my mom, and she gets a little confused sometimes."

"I know," Rosita said. "She's scared, too."

"Help her out to the car, okay? We have to get out of here. Then we'll get you back to your parents. Just as soon as we can."

Rosita's eyes lit up a little. "Okay."

Leah returned to see that Hallie was already tying Krantz to the table. "Nice work," she told Hallie. "I doubt he'll try to go anywhere with that leg of his, but it's good to be safe."

"If the door's locked, he'll be stuck in here anyway," Hallie pointed out. "Since he won't have his keys."

"Let's go." Leah headed for the door.

"Should we turn off the light?"

Leah shrugged. "Nah. Let him enjoy this lovely place he created." She slammed the heavy door shut, waiting as Jon turned the keys in the locks. Then they hurried out of the compound area, and Jon locked the gate. Leah could hear her mom sobbing in the car. In the backseat with Rosita, Ellen was close to hysteria now. "Hallie, you sit in front so I can sit with my mom," Leah told her. "I'll try to calm her down."

"And I want everyone to stay down low," Jon said as he started the engine. "In case there's anyone out there with a gun pointed our way."

"But won't they assume Krantz is driving—" Leah suddenly realized the driver's-side window was missing, leaving Jon completely exposed. "Oh, yeah, I guess they'll see you, huh?"

"Pretty much."

Leah put her arms around her mother, pulling her close and rocking her like a little child as Ellen continued to sob quietly. "It's going to be okay, Mom," Leah reassured her. "You're going home now."

"Home?"

"Yeah," Leah said, trying not to remember the home she'd grown up in—just her and her mom. "Back to The Willows."

"Willows?" Her mom sounded a tiny bit hopeful.

"And we'll get you some ice cream," Leah said enticingly. That was her mom's favorite treat.

"Ice cream?"

"Yeah. With bananas and chocolate sauce." Leah

gently stroked her mom's short blond hair. "And your friends will be there, and everything will be okay."

"Okay," she mumbled, starting to relax in Leah's arms.

Leah could hear the police radio running up in front, but the volume was low and she didn't really understand the code language anyway. "Do you know what they're talking about?" she quietly asked Jon.

"Sounds like trouble," he told her.

"What do you mean?"

"Road block up ahead."

"A road block?" Leah tried to keep her voice calm. "But how do the police know we're in a vehicle?"

"I'm guessing Krantz's buddy got word to the cops somehow. Sounds like they know we're driving his car. They're on the lookout for us."

"At least Krantz won't be with them. That's one less bad cop," she reasoned. "Maybe the roadblock is being manned by some honest cops, Jon. Maybe we could just surrender to them and—"

"I'm not sure we want to take that chance, Leah. Not without some backup from state police or someone we can trust. Even a so-called good cop will be under the impression that we're dangerous criminals. If Krantz's buddy got to them, they know I shot a cop. That's not good." He was driving much slower now.

"What'll we do?"

"I'm trying to think."

"Hey, I noticed a beach access trail that cut into this road," she said suddenly. "It's easy to miss, but should be near here. Unless we passed it already."

"I didn't notice any access to the beach."

"But if we find it, couldn't we drive on the beach?" she asked. "Miss the roadblock?"

"Beach driving won't be easy since it's high tide right now. But it might be safer than the road." He slowed the car down even more. "I think I see a place where the road widens a little. Is that it?"

She peered over the back of the front seat. "I think so."

"Is everyone buckled into a seat belt?" he asked. "This is going to be a bumpy ride."

Leah buckled her mom's seat belt.

"Hold on," Jon called as he went down the beach access road.

Leah wrapped her arms around her mom's shoulders, trying to make it seem like this was a fun trip. "We're going to take a moonlight ride on the beach," she said cheerfully as they bumped along.

The ride grew less bone-jarring as Jon drove the car along the beach. "I'm going to turn off the headlights," he announced after a bit. "In case anyone happens to be looking down here."

Leah could still hear the coded chatter on the police band radio and although she couldn't make out most of it, she did catch some. "Are they saying we *killed* Krantz?" she whispered to Jon.

"Sounds like it. His buddy must've got back to the cops somehow."

"But they'll eventually find out he's wrong. Krantz is alive."

"He was alive when we left him." Jon made a shush

sound, turning the radio's volume up slightly. Leah strained her ears to listen but still wasn't quite making sense of the jabber.

"It gets even better," Jon said sarcastically.

"What?"

"We're the ones suspected of trafficking now—both humans and drugs. Armed and dangerous cop killers and traffickers to boot. No wonder they've got roadblocks. And not just up by the cabins, either. Along the highway out of town, too. They're probably all wearing riot gear and bearing high-powered automatic weapons."

"We've got to get the word out to some good law enforcement," Leah said weakly. "Make them understand. There must be some good cops out there somewhere, Jon. Ones not involved in Krantz's dirty schemes."

"Even so, the ones around here are assuming the worst about us. And anyway, we know there must be a few other cops involved with Krantz and his trafficking schemes." Jon shook his head. "And how do we know who's good and who isn't?" He sighed. "And does it even matter?"

Leah nudged Hallie on the shoulder. "Have there been others involved in kidnapping? I mean other cops that you know of?"

"There are three cops," Hallie said solemnly. "Three that I know about anyway."

"And the guy with Krantz tonight? Was he one of them?" Jon asked.

"I never saw that guy before."

"So then there are at least four involved in trafficking?" Leah had never questioned the police in Cape Perpetua before. Never had cause to. Was it possible that everyone on the force was crooked? It seemed unlikely.

"Uh-oh," Jon said quietly.

"Uh-oh—*what*?" Leah asked.

"Up ahead on the beach. Do you see that?"

Leah peered over the back of the front seat again, but saw nothing but darkness up ahead. She looked down at the phone that she'd been hoping to get connectivity with, but it was still useless.

"It's a cop car!" Hallie's voice was filled with fear. "On the beach."

"Looks like there are two of them," Jon confirmed. "About a mile or so past my parents' cabin. They've blockaded the beach."

"They don't want us to get out of here," Leah said quietly, trying not to upset her mom, who was already trembling.

"They'll never let us go," Rosita sobbed. "Never!"

"They're gonna kill us," Hallie said in a calm but chilling tone. "Just like they said they would do—if we ran."

FIFTEEN

"What'll we do?" Leah quietly asked Jon. She was still holding her mother and trying to comfort Rosita. But it did not look good.

"We can't drive any farther—not without being spotted. For all I know the guys on the beach have already seen us." Jon had already turned the car toward the bluff, driving between pieces of driftwood in an attempt to conceal the vehicle.

"Maybe we should turn back," Leah said.

"I'd considered going toward the jetty earlier." Jon sounded discouraged and weary. "But I was worried about getting us out on foot over that rough terrain. This seemed the best option. Maybe it was a mistake."

"I'm sure the cops are down by the jetty, too," Leah told him.

"I need to get this car out of sight." The tires were having difficulty in the soft sand as he attempted to maneuver it closer to the bluff. "If that's even possible."

"And then what?" Leah asked.

"Maybe we could send your mom and the girls out on foot," he suggested. "They could walk down the beach, approaching the cops with their hands in the air. And once they got close enough, one of them—probably Hallie—could explain what's really going on."

"No way!" Hallie protested. "I don't trust the cops. There's no way I'll give myself up to them."

"No way," Rosita echoed. "Cops are bad. They'll hurt us."

"Not all cops are bad," Jon tried.

"No!" Hallie declared hotly. "I won't do it. You promised to get us to safety."

Leah suddenly realized something. Leaning over the seat, she spoke quietly to Jon. "These girls and my mom are *eyewitnesses* to the crimes that Krantz has pulled off. If even one of those cops is in cahoots with Krantz, these girls' lives are in as much danger as ours."

"You're right." Jon turned off the engine. "I hadn't really considered that. The last thing Krantz wants is for us to get out of this alive."

"Any of us," she said quietly as they all got out of the car.

Jon removed the rifle and the revolver, handing the smaller gun to Leah. "Just in case," he said. "The safety is on. But be careful with it just the same."

Leah wasn't sure she wanted to carry the firearm, but understood his thinking as she zipped it into the pocket that didn't contain the phone.

"Maybe we can find shelter in one of the cabins." Jon frowned up at the bluff. "Not my parents' place, since they might've figured that out by now."

Leah wondered how Ralph was doing, but knew that there was nothing she could do. He was probably better off than the rest of them. "Come on, Mom." She took her mom's hand, encouraging her to walk. "We're going to have a little stroll on the beach now."

"Where am I?" Her mom didn't budge as she looked all around in confusion.

"On the beach, Mom. Can you hear the ocean?"

Her mom frowned as if listening, then nodded. "Where are we going?"

"Someplace nice." Leah tried to sound cheerful as she chattered at her mom, getting her to slowly move her feet through the loose dry sand. Praying that those cop cars on the beach weren't using any special night vision or sound equipment right now.

Suddenly she noticed that Jon had lagged considerably behind them. He was having a hard time with his bad leg, even trying to use the rifle as a cane, which seemed a little dangerous. Leah quietly called Rosita back to her. "Can you please walk with Ellen so that Hallie and I can help Jon?"

"Okay." Rosita took the older woman's hand. "Come on, Ellen, let's go."

"Don't get too far ahead," Leah warned. "If you see or hear anything suspicious, run back to us fast." Leah considered their two firearms, wondering if they'd actually need to use them again. She hoped not. It was one thing going after Krantz, a known criminal, but the last thing she wanted was to risk shooting a cop who wasn't aligned with Krantz. That was downright disturbing.

Leah rejoined Jon. "I'll carry the rifle," she said as she wrapped her other arm around his waist. Hallie was already on the other side, and together they helped him limp up the beach.

"It's not too far from here," Jon huffed. "I just thought of a good cabin for us."

"And once everyone's settled, I can climb that rock again," Leah suggested. "The one where you sometimes get phone connectivity. Only this time, I won't try to call. I'll just send my text to everyone and anyone—state police, FBI, even the local precinct. I'll even send it to some friends and my great-aunt. I'll get it ready in the house, then sneak out and—"

"The area will be crawling with cops," he reminded her.

"I'll be careful. And I'll have it all ready to send so I won't have to talk."

"It's a good idea. But the cabin we're going to borrow is pretty swanky, Leah. It might even have a landline."

"A landline!" Leah felt her hopes rising.

"There's a rickety stairway along here somewhere," he explained. "It's been roped off because it needs to be replaced, but it leads up to the Malcolms' cabin. I don't know why I didn't think of the Malcolm place before." He exhaled loudly. "Except I wasn't much into breaking and entering before."

"Funny what one does to keep from getting killed these days," Leah said drily.

"The Malcolms are my parents' friends," he huffed. "They'll understand."

"Even if there's no landline, we can hole up there while I send a text." Leah tried to sound optimistic.

"Will they have food there?" Hallie asked hopefully.

"Probably," Jon told her. "And under the circumstances, I'm sure they'll be happy to share."

"Can you even make it up stairs with your leg?" Leah quietly asked him. From what she could tell, Jon could barely walk now.

"I'll have to."

"We'll help you," Hallie assured him.

"We must be close now." Jon paused to catch his breath, looking up the dark bluff, then over to the beach where the cop cars were still parked—and not that far away. Leah followed his gaze, noticing how they were now using searchlights to sweep back and forth across the sand. Was it possible the cops knew they were nearby? What if Krantz's car had some kind of tracking device?

"That's it," Jon said quietly, pointing to what looked like a faded sign hanging on a piece of rope that cordoned off a dilapidated set of beach access stairs.

"Danger. Do Not Enter." Rosita read the words.

"Sounds like the past twenty-four hours," Leah said as she stepped over the rope. "I'll test the stairs first. Just to be sure we really want to attempt this."

"Be careful," Jon warned.

"Do you still have your flashlight?" Leah asked as she handed him back the rifle.

"Yeah." He fished it out. "Keep the beam low. In case the cops look this way."

"I want to use it to check the stairs," she explained. "Might want to see what we're walking on."

"Good idea."

With the others huddled down below, Leah stepped onto the first step. Hearing it creak beneath her weight, she used the flashlight to examine the condition. Of course, the stairs were bad. Not to mention slick and rickety, but after going about halfway up, she decided they might hold. She prayed they would.

When she got back down, she suggested that Rosita, being the lightest one, go up first. "Walk very carefully and use the railing," Leah warned the girl. "Remember the steps are slick." She placed a hand on Rosita's shoulder. "Walk very gently and then wait for us on top."

Rosita nodded. "Okay."

"And I'll send Ellen after you. When she gets to the top, can you help her not to be too scared? Maybe hold her hand?"

"I'll do that." Rosita reached for the handrail, then slowly started up the stairs.

Leah turned to her mom now. "You'll follow Rosita," she said calmly. "Just take your time. And let's play a little game."

"A game?"

"Yes. You must walk as quietly as a mouse."

Her mom looked slightly confused, but nodded. "A mouse?"

"Almost your turn now." Leah led her mom to the stairs and when she felt sure that Rosita was at the top, she guided her mom's hand to the railing. "Use the handrail. And careful mouse footsteps. Okay?"

"Okay."

"You'll be home soon," Leah reassured Ellen as she gingerly set foot onto the first step. Leah prayed for her safety as she watched her disappearing into the darkness of the bluff up above. Listening to hear if there was any problem, she kept one hand on the railing, feeling the vibrations of each step. And finally, satisfied that her mom was at the top, Leah turned to Hallie. "You go next. Walk gently."

"What about Jon?" Hallie asked. "Do you need me to help you with—"

"No," Jon firmly said. "I'll be fine. You just keep Rosita and Ellen quiet when you get up there, Hallie. And wait for Leah to join you before going into the house."

After Hallie was partway up, Leah turned to Jon. "I'll help you—"

"No. You've been doing this just right, Leah. I doubt the stairs are strong enough for both of us. Your turn."

"But you need—"

"Go, Leah," he commanded. "I'll use the railing like a cane. I can do this. Just go—*now*!"

Leah started to argue, but could tell by his expression it was pointless. "Be careful," she warned.

"If anything happens to me, just keep going with the plan you made," he said.

"No. I'll come back to—"

"I mean it, Leah. Promise me you'll get the others into the Malcolm house. Try to be quiet when you break in. As soon as you get the others safely inside—look for a landline."

"Okay." Certain Hallie was on top now, Leah started her second trek up the slick rickety stairs. With the rifle in one hand, she used the other hand to hold on to the railing and tried to be as light-footed as possible. Even so, it seemed that the whole structure was swaying beneath her weight—even more than she recalled from her first attempt. She felt amazed that the others had made it safely to the top and wondered what she would do if the whole thing gave way. And even if it held for her, what about Jon? He was the heaviest one of the bunch, not to mention unstable on his feet. *God help us*, she prayed.

Her mind continued racing with each careful step. Even if they did make it up—and if they did break into the Malcolm cabin without being seen or heard— unless there was a landline there, what good would it do them? And if it was such a nice cabin, wouldn't it have a security system like Jon's parents' cabin? She hadn't voiced these doubts to Jon. It seemed pointless. But if a security alarm went off, it wouldn't take long for the cops to figure out that they were holed up inside. And what then? Exchanging gunfire? She didn't think so.

As her feet hit the solid ground at the top of the bluff Leah felt surprised and relieved that the stairway was still intact. Everything in her wanted to stay here to help Jon, even if only to encourage him from a distance. But she remembered her promise. She needed to get her mom and the girls into the house.

"Come on," she told the three of them as she led the way down a trail of pave stones. "It looks like this will get us there." Soon they were clustered in a small courtyard, a bit bigger than the one at Jon's parents' cabin. Leah cautiously looked around, hoping there were no nosy cops sniffing around. Feeling they were not being watched, she tried to decide how to get in the tall darkened house looming before them.

As she went closer, she could see that the back door was half glass window. Praying there was no alarm system in place, she removed the velour warm-up jacket and emptied the pockets, wrapping the soft fabric around the sturdy stock of the rifle. Then, holding it up like she'd seen in movies, she gouged the padded gun stock through the window part of the door. Her hopes that the fabric might muffle the noise were dashed as the sound of a dull thud and the tinkle of breaking glass cut into the otherwise quiet evening.

Praying that no one was close enough to hear, she reached through the broken window to unlock the door. Holding her breath, she listened for the shrill cries of an alarm. What would they do if it sounded? Run? Hide? Where?

To her relief, all she could hear was the sound of the surf behind her as she opened the door. Still, she knew some systems were silent. Right now, the cops could be getting a phone call from the security company—preparing to apprehend them.

"Go inside," she quietly commanded the girls and her mom. Waiting as they passed through the door, she couldn't stop thinking about Jon. As difficult as walking had been for him, it would be next to impossible for him to climb those stairs. She needed to help him.

And yet, remembering her promise, she knew she had to at least get the others to a safe spot—and attempt to locate a landline. That was her best hope. "Don't turn on any lights," she warned them. "The cops are probably nearby and lights would get their attention." She made her way through what appeared to be, based on the limited light from outside, the kitchen. She tried a nearby door and discovered a pitch-black room that seemed to contain laundry facilities. Suspecting by the darkness that there were no windows, she turned the flashlight on, pointing it downward. No windows.

"Come in here," she told the others. "It's not a big space, but I'll leave you the flashlight and since there aren't windows, you can leave it on. Just be quiet, okay?"

Once they were huddled in the room, Leah gave Rosita charge of the flashlight, and not wanting to lug the rifle around, she slipped it behind the washing machine. "Turn it off if you hear anyone else in the house, okay? They might see the beam beneath the door."

Hallie nodded with a serious expression.

"I'm going to look for a phone," she said. "I'll be back soon. With food and water, too."

Still worried about Jon and thinking he should be here by now, although she knew his leg would slow him down considerably, she began the search for a phone. The kitchen seemed the best place to start and, sure enough, she found one with a cord that was attached to the wall. But when she held it to her ear—nothing. She tried pushing buttons, but still nothing. It was dead. Probably disconnected.

Feeling seriously worried about Jon, she went to the back door, ready to run to his aid. As she ventured outside, she listened intently to the reassuring sound of the ocean waves. She was just heading down the path to the bluff when a dull cracking noise sent a shiver of fear through her. It was followed by the sounds of creaking, breaking, crumbling and crashing. She knew that the bulky wooden structure had tumbled onto the rocks below. The stairway had failed. And Jon was on it!

SIXTEEN

Using his good leg, Jon leaped for solid ground just as the rickety stairway crashed to the rocks below—making enough noise to draw unwanted attention.

Knowing the cops could be here any moment, he struggled to his feet. He had to get to cover! Unable to run, he limped clumsily, dragging his bad leg down the path toward the Malcolm place when he heard the sound of footsteps running. Bracing himself for the worst, he looked for a place to hide—then realized it was Leah!

She immediately threw her arms around him. "You're okay," she whispered as she began helping him toward the cabin. "I was so scared. I thought you were goners on that stairway."

"The stairway is gone." He leaned into her, trying to move faster, but enjoying the closeness of her next to him. "Did you break in?"

"Mom and the girls are inside. As far as I can see there's not an alarm system, either."

"Good news."

"And I found a landline, but it's not connected."

"Bad news."

"Come on." She tightened her hold around his waist, trying to move them faster. "Let's get inside."

"Yeah." He tried not to groan in pain, but it felt as if someone had slipped hot coals and sharp knives beneath that bandage.

"You kept the lights off?"

"Yes. I left them in the laundry room. No window."

She paused to open the back door. "Here we are."

He felt the glass crunching beneath his shoes. "You're getting to be quite the break-in artist. Maybe if the nursing thing doesn't work out—"

"Very funny." She closed the door behind them. "I want to clean up that glass just in case a cop comes by." She guided him through the dark room that was probably a kitchen. "That door goes to the laundry room. Do you want to go in there while I clean up the glass and block the door with something?"

"You might as well leave the glass," he said. "One look at the broken window and they'll know we're in here. You still have the guns?"

"Yeah." She held up the revolver. "But I really don't know how to use it. Don't want to use it."

"And you shouldn't. But where's the rifle?"

"I'll get it."

"I want to position myself somewhere I can keep an eye on the front and back doors." He balanced himself against the counter. "That way I can warn you if I think they're onto us."

Leah tapped on the laundry room door. "It's just me," she said quietly. "Turn off the light so I can come in."

He scoped out the house while she went into the laundry room. He could hear the murmuring sound of voices and it was obvious the girls and her mother were frightened. Who could blame them?

Jon finally decided the heavy table between the kitchen and great room was the best place to position himself. He could see both doors and many of the windows. He eased himself onto a stool, using a second stool to elevate his throbbing leg.

When Leah emerged, she handed him the rifle, which he laid across the table. "Do you really plan to use it?" she asked with a concerned frown.

"Not to kill anyone," he explained. "Especially since it's difficult to tell the bad guys from the good. But I'll use it to hold off Krantz's cohorts."

"I need to get the girls and my mom some food and water," she told Jon. "And some blankets to make them comfortable. We don't want anyone going into shock."

"Good thinking." He sat down in one of the swivel stools that surrounded the table. "Think I'll stay here. Good spot to watch everything. But I think you should stay in the laundry room, Leah. Just to be safe."

"I'll figure that out later," Leah told him as she went to work, first getting everyone a glass of water. Then she went through a pantry until she rounded up some crackers, a jar of olives, some Vienna sausages, cans of sardines, bottles of fruit juice, packaged cookies and a few other things, which she distributed to Jon and the others in the laundry room.

After that, she scurried around the house, gathering up some blankets and pillows that she ran to the laundry, too, and like a mother, she reminded them to keep their voices quiet in there. Then she started going through kitchen drawers again.

"You remind me of the Energizer Bunny," he told her. "I don't know how you do it, Leah."

"It helps not having a shot-up leg."

"You need to eat something, too," Jon pointed out.

"I know." She reached for a Vienna sausage, then opened another kitchen drawer.

"What are you looking for?" he asked as he munched a fig bar.

"A phone book. Hopefully one with a government-listings page. I want to plug all the correct numbers into my text messages before I go out to the rock. That way they'll get sent automatically. You know?"

Jon grimaced. He really didn't like the idea of her going out there by herself, but he knew it was probably their best hope now. "You'll be really careful, won't you?"

"Of course. But I think I should get right to it, Jon. No time to waste. Before they figure out we're here."

"I agree."

"Bingo," she said as she held something up. "I'll take the phone book to the laundry room so I can use the flashlight to see."

"Before you go," Jon said suddenly, "can you find me a paper and a pen? I want to write a note to put on the back door. In case the police come. In case there's an honest one among them. I want to explain what's going on in here. Why we have your mom and the girls—and Krantz's role in this."

"Good idea, Jon." She went back to rummage through drawers, quickly locating a tablet and pen as well as some Scotch tape. "Can you see to write it without light?" She laid it in front of him.

"It won't be easy, but I'll try to make it legible."

After Leah went into the laundry room, he attempted to write his note. Being an artist, he had pretty good penmanship. Still, he didn't know what good it would do. But if an honest cop was the one to find and read it, it might help. And despite Hallie and Rosita's convictions that there was no such thing as an honest cop in this town, he knew that was only based on their experience with three bad ones. Those had to be the exception. He also knew that even an honest cop could be dangerous if he thought he was going up against cop-killing criminals. It was simply the way they were trained. Jon understood and respected this.

But somehow he had to convince whoever read this note that they were innocent victims—and that Krantz was not. And in just a few words, too. If he'd ever needed good attorney skills, it was now. He wadded up his first attempt, then launched into another. He had just finished what seemed like a convincing letter when Leah emerged from the laundry room.

"All quiet on the western front?" she whispered.

"No sign of anyone or anything out there." He frowned. "Surprising, considering the noise that crumbling stairway must've made."

"God is helping us," she told him.

"I hope so. We need it."

"I got what I need all ready to be sent from your

phone," she said. "And I also learned the names of the other two cops that were helping Krantz. First names anyway. Brett and Gordie. And Krantz's first name is Erik."

"Brett and Gordie and Erik." Jon jotted the names down on the pad.

"And she told me that she found the names of several other girls. They were written on one of the walls."

"Kidnapped girls?"

"That's what Hallie thought. A couple of the names sounded familiar."

"The ones my mom had been researching?" he asked eagerly.

She nodded. "I put them in the phone, too."

"We should write it all down, too," he said. "Just in case."

"I'll ask Hallie to do that." Leah took a sip of water. "Oh, there's something else," she said suddenly. "Hallie told me that they're smuggling drugs, too. She heard someone say that they come in by boat from Mexico."

"It figures." He let out a deep sigh.

"Well, no time to waste, right?" she said brightly. Almost as if she were looking forward to this.

"Just be careful." He held up his note. "And put this by the back door, okay?"

She took the page from him, then leaned over, whispering in his ear. "And just in case something happens…it's been nice knowing you, Jon Wilson."

"Oh, Leah, don't talk like that." He reached over to touch her cheek, amazed at how smooth it was.

"Well, anything could happen. You know that, Jon."

"I know. But I really want to see you again." There was so much more he wanted to say…so many words that felt stuck inside him. Would he ever get the chance? "Please, be careful out there."

"I will." She suddenly wrapped her arms around his neck, laying her head on his shoulder. "You, too. If they come knocking, please, don't have a shoot-out."

"I won't." As she was pulling away, he reached for her face, pulling it toward him. "Leah," he whispered. "There's still so much I want to say to you, when there's time." And then, for the second time, he kissed her. And this kiss wasn't just in passing, either. Not a fluke. This time he kissed her with an intensity that he hoped she would understand. He wanted her to know that his feelings for her were real. He was even tempted to use the *L* word—*love*—yet the timing seemed less than ideal. "If anything happens to you, I'll—"

"It won't," she assured him as she picked up his note. "I'll be very, very careful, and I'm *fast*. I'll be back in less than five minutes, Jon." She placed a hand on his shoulder. "Unless something goes wrong."

He groaned. "Don't say that."

"I mean if someone is out there," she reassured him. "I might have to wait. If I'm not back in five minutes, don't worry. It'll just mean that I'm being very, very careful. Okay?"

"Okay." He nodded with uncertainty. "Just be safe. That's all that matters."

She hurried to the back door, taping the note onto the outside of it before she slipped out, quietly closing the door after her. Disappearing into the night.

Even though Jon knew that the girls and Leah's mom were nearby, still cloistered in the laundry room and whispering quietly to each other as they dined on their pantry picnic, he had never felt this alone before. It was as if Leah's departure had taken everything good about life with her. As if there was nothing left without her. It was such an overwhelming feeling, he could hardly contain it. As if his life had lost its meaning without her.

He didn't know what he'd do if she didn't return… if anything happened to her. He couldn't bear to think about it. And wished he could do something about it. But with his leg messed up like this, there was little he could do to help her. He didn't like feeling this helpless. It wasn't who he was. He remembered when he'd jumped on Krantz to help Leah, how strong and capable he'd felt. Although look where that had gotten him. At the moment, he wouldn't be able to defend himself against an aggressive flea. Right now about the only thing he could do was to pray. Pray and hold the fort. If that were even possible.

After an earnest prayer he decided to write another note to post on the front door, if only to distract himself from worry. Leah could tape it up when she returned, or else he'd hobble over and do it himself. As he carefully scribed one similar to the other note, he chided himself. Why hadn't he done this yesterday—when they were at his parents' cabin? Maybe they'd be safe by now.

Except that if they'd been rescued, they never would've located Leah's mom and the girls. Or, more likely, Krantz would've found and destroyed the note before anyone else had a chance to see it.

When Jon finished his second note, he felt certain that at least five minutes had gone by. More like ten. But Leah still hadn't returned. On high alert, he looked out toward the front of the house. He hadn't even noticed any lights going down the road. What was going on out there? Why would it take her so long? She was simply going to climb the rock and send the texts—that would take mere seconds—then sprint back here. Five minutes was plenty of time. After all, Leah was fast.

Unless she'd run into someone. He knew that was possible. What if she'd been found by one of Krantz's buddies? Jon put his hand on the rifle. A lot of good that did him in here. He was no help to Leah. Oh, why had he let her go? Why hadn't he insisted she remain here with him? They could've waited to see if his notes worked. Where was she anyway?

He was just about to get to his feet—not that it would do any good—when he heard the sound of gunshots. Three in quick sequence—*bam-bam-bam*—as if being shot from an automatic weapon. As if the shooter were sure of his target. And then nothing but silence—as if the bullets had hit their mark.

Jon leaned his head onto the granite countertop, biting back bitter tears as the possibilities assaulted him. Leah had been shot—that was the only explanation. She'd been spotted on her way to or from the rock and a cop—probably one with better aim than Krantz—had shot her. As much as he didn't want to believe this, it seemed the only logical explanation. Leah had been shot. *Please, God, don't let her be dead.*

SEVENTEEN

Leah had been hiding in a brushy area near the big rock for nearly ten minutes when she heard voices shouting. She couldn't make out the words. Three shots rang out in succession, sending a chill down her spine. What was going on? Her first thoughts went to Jon. Had he made some sort of heroic effort after she'd left? Possibly turning himself in, hoping that he'd run into a good cop? Only to be disappointed?

She couldn't think about that. She had to get to the top of that rock. And she had to do it from the back, which was steeper than the way she and Jon had climbed it the other time. But from the back side, she felt somewhat sure that she wouldn't be spotted. Especially if they continued to be distracted by whatever had happened on the road. *Please, God, don't let it be Jon*, she silently prayed as she started scaling the rock.

Her elective rock-climbing class came in handy as she felt her way up the massive rock, praying that once she reached the top there would really be connectivity. The fact that this wasn't a foggy night seemed to play in her favor—not in regard to visibility, but the phone connectivity should be better. She paused, clinging to the back side of the rock and listening to the sounds of men shouting down below her. They were obviously excited about something. She hoped it wasn't her.

Finally, nearly to the top, she clung to the ledge of the rock, barely able to peer over the top. The rock towered a good twenty feet over the roofs of the nearby houses and from her vantage point, she could clearly see the headlights of cars and several officers, armed with rifles, mulling about on the road below her. Her blood ran cold as she saw that they had gathered around what appeared to be a slain figure lying lifelessly on the road. That explained the gunshots. *Please, God, don't let it be Jon.*

Holding the phone close to her chest, she peered down, seeing that it showed one bar of connectivity. One bar! Hopefully that was all it would take. She held the phone out a bit, keeping the face of it pointed to the sky, in case anyone was looking from below. And holding her breath and counting to thirty, she prayed that the text messages she had carefully constructed, then attached to phone numbers, were on their way. Praying that whoever was receiving these messages would take them seriously—would send out help.

When she finally pulled the phone down, she was relieved that the texts appeared to have been sent. She was tempted to stick around to see if anyone responded, but knew she had to get back to the Malcolm cabin. If Jon had been shot—and she didn't know if she could bear losing him—her mom and the girls would need her help. More than ever.

As she worked her way down the rock, partly climbing, partly sliding, she heard the sound of footsteps nearby. And as soon as her feet hit the ground, she knew by the speed of the footsteps—getting closer—that she'd been spotted.

"Freeze—hands in the air!" a male voice yelled. "Or I'll shoot."

Leah ducked her head as she leaped for the shadows, and the sound of a gunshot made her run even faster until she saw what looked like an opening in the hedge. Without wasting a moment, she pushed her way through what she hoped was an overgrown beach access trail going down to the ocean, but after just a few feet she realized there was nothing there—just the bluff dropping about thirty feet down to the beach. Feeling her feet sliding over the crumbling edge, she grabbed onto the bushes, which tore off, then she desperately clawed in the rock and sand, trying not to fall over the edge. Her legs dangling down, she tried to pull herself back up, knowing that whoever had just shot at her would probably be up there to greet her with a loaded gun.

But it was useless and as her grip began slipping, she braced herself for a painful fall when she suddenly felt something beneath her feet. A ledge of some sort beneath the cliff. Working to get her feet solidly under her, she slid down the side of the rocky bluff. The ledge was only a few inches wide, not even big enough for her to stand flat-footed. But at least it felt solid. Clinging to the side of the bluff like an insect, she took some deep steadying breaths and listened to what was going on up above her.

She could hear muffled voices, obviously looking for her but seemingly unaware that she'd slipped through the hedge—probably because it looked impossible due to the drop-off below. Knowing she couldn't perch on the narrow ledge for long—already her calf muscles were starting to ache from standing on her tiptoes— she once again employed her rock-climbing skills, rusty though they were, as she eased herself slowly down the concave rock wall.

After about six feet, she came to what felt like a narrow cave carved into the side of the bluff. Thankful for a place to rest and think, she crouched down in the narrow crevice and waited…listening for the searchers up above her…watching as their flashlight beams came through the hedge above, sweeping the beach as they continued their relentless search.

Feeling hopeless and like a hunted animal, Leah was trying not to cry. She leaned into the wall and prayed silently and feverishly for Jon and her mother and the girls—begging God to do something to stop this never-ending madness. Even as she prayed, her mind dredged up an image that seemed to be indelibly printed into her brain—that of the slain man on the road. Was that Jon? Who else could it have been? And if he'd been shot, was he dead? If Krantz's cohorts had anything to say about it, he would be dead.

This realization made her feel sick inside—how could it be that after all they'd been through, after she'd possibly gotten the text messages sent, it would end like this? Her body ached all over and she felt too weak to go on. How would she ever survive this mess without Jon by her side? It felt impossible. And impossibly cruel. Would God really allow that to happen? Would God take him like that? Allow her to fall for him and then just take him away? Snatch him up even before she had the chance to express her true feelings to him?

Why hadn't she told Jon how she felt? What had she been waiting for? Why had she been playing it so cautiously? And why had she obsessed over Monica? Especially after Jon had told her it was all behind him? Why hadn't she believed him and let it go? Why hadn't she told him she loved him? Because it was true—she did love him. She knew it!

And, yet, even if she had confessed her love—what difference would it make now? If Jon were dead—what would it matter? What did anything matter? Except that he could've died knowing that she loved him. Perhaps that would've made it easier. Or not.

She took in a deep breath, listening intently, wondering if the cops were still up above her. But it was very quiet, almost as if they'd given up. Or were looking elsewhere for her. With only the sound of the ocean waves, Leah knew what she had to do. If Jon really had been shot—her mom and the girls would be alone. She needed to get back to them, to wait and hope that the text messages had achieved their purpose.

Hopefully the police didn't know they were holed up at the Malcolms'. If they knew, Leah would have little chance of getting back into that house. But she needed to at least try. And that meant climbing the rest of the way down this bluff—hopefully without plummeting straight down. She suspected she had at least a twenty-foot drop remaining—too far to jump safely onto the sand. Leah eased herself over the edge of the precipice where she'd been hiding. Feeling with her toes, trying to find footholds, she hoped that this whole wall wasn't concave.

To her relief, as she swung slightly, her feet came in contact with some toeholds. Getting firm handholds, she gingerly made her way down. It felt as if it took forever and the whole while she braced herself for the exposing beam of a high-powered flashlight coming from the beach where the cop cars were probably still parked. Probably with their high-powered rifles ready to shoot. But when she finally put her feet on soft sand, she realized she had made it.

But now what? She leaned against the bluff wall, trying to make a decision. At last, she decided her best choice might be to go down to the stairs that belonged to Jon's parents' cabin, and to make her way up there and back toward the Malcolms'.

Leah walked along the sand, staying close to the darkness of the bluff wall. As she went, she spotted the cop cars still blockading the beach. Fortunately, they didn't seem too intent on using their searchlights. She wondered if they'd even spotted Krantz's car yet. But she didn't want to take the time to investigate. The more she thought about her mom and the girls, the faster she wanted to go. If anything happened to them…well, she didn't even know what she'd do.

It wasn't long until she reached the stone beach steps,

but knowing there could be a cop posted at the top of these stairs, she paused to think. It felt as if all her options were disintegrating—as if she were a hunted animal with no place left to hide. And so she started up, trying to move silently. She didn't know what else to do. She felt so tired and discouraged—and sick about possibly losing Jon—that she almost didn't care anymore. If they were going to catch her and kill her, let them. Just get it over with. Maybe it would be for the best.

Even so, she went up cautiously, listening with each step, and praying for God's protection. When she reached the top step, she was relieved and somewhat shocked to discover no one around. Was she really out of harm's way?

She was about to head on up to the Malcolm cabin when she noticed the beam of a searchlight sweeping across the top of the bluff—in the same direction she wanted to go. They were obviously still looking for her. And so, instead of proceeding to the Malcolm cabin, she let herself into the back door of Jon's parents' place. She didn't know why or what she would do there, but it was close—and it was shelter.

She knew that Krantz and some of his buddies had already searched the cabin, and it seemed possible they wouldn't come back here. As she went inside, she remembered poor little Ralph. Was he still locked in the upstairs bedroom? And what if he heard her and barked? She could be setting her own trap.

Just the same she continued, feeling her way through the darkened house. She crept silently up the stairs and then, as she approached the door to the little bedroom, she spoke in a calm, gentle tone, praying Ralph would keep quiet.

As she turned the doorknob, she heard a low growling—the sound a dog makes right before it starts barking. "It's okay, boy," she continued talking soothingly. "It's just me. Hey, Ralphie."

As she went into the dark room, she heard him coming toward her. Kneeling, she reached for him. "Oh, you poor little guy." She scooped him up, holding him close. Suddenly she remembered that sunny day she'd been running and the way Ralph had happily run along with her. She remembered how attractive Ralph's master had looked with his sandy hair blowing in the breeze, the look of intensity in his dark brown eyes. It had felt as if it were meant to be when their paths had crossed on the beach. She put her face into Ralph's coat, trying not to cry as she wondered if she'd ever see Jon again.

"We didn't leave you for good," she whispered hoarsely. "Not on purpose."

She fumbled in the dark until she found the candle and matches and then, after lighting it, she refilled Ralph's water bowl and put a few spoonfuls of dog food out, as well. "Sorry to leave you again." She set the bowls before him, gently petting him. "But as soon as we're safe, you'll be safe, too."

She secured his bandage better as he lapped up some water. "You keep resting," she whispered, knowing she couldn't spend too much time here. There were still her mom and the girls to think of. Seeing that Ralph was settled down, she blew out the candle. "Hopefully help will be here soon. And you'll see your master again."

As she said this, hot tears slipped down her cheeks. Really, what was the likelihood of this? And what was the likelihood she would escape this nightmare alive? By the time she left this cabin, the cops could be waiting outside for her, guns aimed at her head. If it was the bad cops, she would probably end up like— She had to stop thinking like this.

For the sake of the girls and her mom, she knew she had to keep fighting. She had to give this her full effort. And if her text messages had actually been sent, it was possible that someone somewhere had already read them, and that help was on its way. She tried to imagine dispatchers sending law enforcement out here, wondering how they would handle it. Really, she told herself as she slipped out the bedroom door, it could happen. She couldn't give up.

She tiptoed back down the stairs and paused to listen in the hallway. Hearing the silence of the house and seeing no sign of anyone, no lights outside, nothing…she cracked open the back door, cautiously peering around before she slipped outside and stealthily began working her way through the neighbors' backyards in the direction of the Malcolm cabin.

Climbing over fences and rock walls, pushing through hedges, she slowly made her way toward the Malcolm house. And yet she knew it might no longer be a secure hideout. By now the police might've discovered where she'd broken into the back door. Perhaps that was why Jon had attempted to make a run for it— to lead the cops away from her mom and the girls. Perhaps he'd sacrificed himself for their safety.

But even if the police had shot and killed Jon, or had him in custody, Leah knew they wouldn't be satisfied until they'd thoroughly searched that cabin. They would easily find the "hostages" in the laundry room. And then what would they do? If it were Krantz's buddies, it would not be good.

As she got closer to the Malcolm cabin, she could hear the sounds of officers out on the road. And in the distance, she could hear the whining sound of a siren. Was that an ambulance coming for the shooting victim? Or could it be one of the law enforcement agencies she'd texted, on their way to help? She wondered how much time had lapsed since she'd sent those texts.

Pausing on a neighboring cabin's patio that overlooked the ocean, she leaned against the house to catch her breath and check her watch. It had been more than twenty minutes since she'd texted. Surely some other form of law enforcement would be on their way by now. Even so, how long would it take them to get here?

Before long, she was at the place where the wooden staircase had fallen, and she knew she was nearly to the Malcolm house. All of a sudden, she heard heavy footsteps coming quickly from behind her. Without hesitating, she broke into a full run for the Malcolm house. As she ran, she saw the beam of a searchlight sweeping across the trail.

"Freeze!" someone shouted. "Hands up! Or I shoot!"

For a split second, she considered obeying, wishing she could surrender to an honest cop—but then Krantz's leering face flashed through her mind and she imagined a bullet ripping through her. The path ahead was about to turn to the Malcolm cabin, and she went for it—full speed, hoping for shelter in the cabin.

More shouts were followed by gunfire as she raced down the trail, knowing her speed could save her. As she reached the Malcolms' courtyard, several more shots rang out in quick sequence. With the door almost in reach, she felt herself going down.

EIGHTEEN

"Get away!" Jon yelled as he fired another warning shot out the back door—aiming more toward the beach than the shooters. "Or I'll shoot again." Then, without hesitation and hoping his leg wouldn't let him down, he leaped through the open back door and grabbed Leah by one limp arm, dragging her seemingly lifeless body into the house and away from the gunfire. Without wasting a second, and using up every last morsel of strength, he shoved the heavy kitchen table up against the compromised door. He knew it wouldn't take a couple of cops long to push the blocked door open, but it might stall them. Perhaps long enough for them to read the note taped to the door.

"Leah?" He bent down, peering into her face and fearing the worst. "Leah, talk to me. Are you okay?"

She opened her eyes, blinking up at him. "Jon? Wh-what happened? Where am I?"

"You're with me, Leah. Where were you shot? Are you in pain?" Although the light in there was dim, he saw no sign of blood pooling on the kitchen floor. "Have you been wounded?"

"I—I don't feel any pain." She reached for his hand, letting him help her to her feet. Still worried about the shooters outside, he moved her well away from the door, wanting to get her far from harm's way, but wondering where that was.

"When I heard those shots—saw you falling—I thought for sure you'd been shot." With the rifle still in one hand, he used his other hand to hold tightly to hers, wishing he could hold on to her forever. "You had me so worried, Leah."

She collapsed in his arms, choking back sobs. "Me, too. I was certain they'd shot you, Jon, but you're alive!"

"And so are you." He hurried to guide her toward the laundry room now, deciding it was the only way to protect her. "You go in there with your mom and the girls while I see if I can reason with the guys outside. I want them to read my note."

"I want to stay with you," she insisted.

"You're shaking," he told her. "You've been through so—"

"I'm okay." She stepped away from him, standing taller. "I'll help you hold them off, Jon." She unzipped her pocket. "I've still got the revolver. Even if I can't hit anything, I can shoot to scare someone if I need to."

"I only shot to make them back off. I don't want it to turn into a shooting match." His eyes remained fixed on the back door with the broken-out window. "But if you're going to stay here with me, help me find a piece of furniture that we can hide behind—just in case."

While Leah went looking for a shield, Jon tried to think of a better plan. He knew the cops were out there, probably strategizing a new plan of attack. Hopefully they wouldn't resort to something like tear gas. There'd be no defense against that. If only he could get an honest cop to talk to him. That could make all the difference. Hearing the sound of something moving behind him, he turned to see Leah pushing a large dining table toward the kitchen.

"How about this for starters?" she asked.

"That might work if we turn it on its side."

"It's solid and heavy," she said as she pushed it toward him.

Together, they turned the massive table over. It was a hefty piece, but he wasn't sure it would stop bullets. Still, it was better than nothing.

"I'll look for something to shield us from the front of the house," Leah said as she went into the living area. "Just in case they break in that way."

"Good thinking." As he slid a pair of the kitchen stools behind the table, Leah returned pushing a leather love seat. Scooting the bulky piece a couple of feet from the table made a small fort, similar to something a child would make. Not exactly bulletproof, but at least it would conceal them.

"If they start to shoot, you drop down out of sight," he instructed. "Better yet, I wish you'd go in the laundry room and wait until—"

"I'm staying here," she said stubbornly. "With you."

"Have it your way." He perched on a stool, resting the rifle barrel over the edge of the overturned table as if he planned to defend them—when in reality he knew he would only fire warning shots. No way was he going to chance killing a cop. He wondered how long the cops would wait outside. Were they scheming a way to flush them out? What if they used explosives?

"What are they doing?" she whispered. "Why is it so quiet out there?"

"I don't know." Hoping to distract her a little, he decided to change the subject. "What made you fall like that when they were shooting?"

"I don't really know." She sighed. "Maybe I blacked out from just plain fear."

"I'd been watching for you at the back door," he told her. "I was so worried, Leah. It had taken too long. And I'd heard those gunshots." He blew out a long sigh. "I honestly thought they'd gotten you. And you were gone for such a long time. I thought you were dead." He wanted to say how frightened he'd been when he'd felt as if he'd lost her, but somehow the words wouldn't come. Maybe it was the wrong time.

"That's what I thought, too," she said urgently. "That they'd shot you, Jon. I heard gunshots while I was on the rock and then I saw a slain man on the road. I thought maybe you'd run outside to keep them from discovering Mom and the girls." She looked over to the laundry room door. "It's so quiet in there. Are they okay?"

"They're fine. I asked them to be quiet. Although I'm sure the gunshots scared them. You could go in there and check on them. Stay awhile." He really wanted to get her to a safe place. If that were possible.

She looked over her shoulder toward the front door. "I really think I'm more useful here, Jon. What if they storm both doors at once?"

"Yeah." He didn't really want to think about that, but knew she was right. "So what happened out there?" he asked. "You say you made it to the rock?"

She quickly explained about having to hide for a while. "It seemed like cops were everywhere. So I climbed up the back side of the rock so they couldn't see me."

"You climbed up the back of the rock? It's practically straight up from that side. Impressive."

"It felt safer, but it took longer. Once I was up there, I got a connection. Just one bar, but enough to send the texts. They went out pretty slowly—but at least they went. And then I heard those three gunshots down on the street. I could see someone down there—I thought for sure it was you."

"That's what I heard, too. Three gunshots." He remembered the shock waves that had run through him when he'd assumed it was Leah. "I didn't know what to do."

"That's how I felt, Jon." Her voice cracked. "It made me sick to think you'd been killed. Such a horrible feeling. I couldn't bear to lose you, Jon. I don't know what I'd do without you." She let out a shaky sigh.

"I know… I felt the same way, Leah." He reached over to touch her cheek, longing to do more. "There's so much I want to say to you. Things I couldn't tell you—if you were…well, you know."

"Dead?" she offered softly.

He set down the rifle, reaching out to take her face in his hands. "If we ever get out of this alive—there's so much I want to say." And now he kissed her, drinking in her sweetness and wishing they'd met under different circumstances. When he released her they just continued gazing into each others' eyes.

"We have to survive this," she said quietly. "I just promised Ralph we'd be back for him."

"Ralph?"

Now she quickly explained about running from someone with a gun, nearly falling off the bluff and eventually winding up in his parents' cabin with Ralph. Jon couldn't believe all she'd been through in the past thirty minutes, but at least she was here now. And still alive. "Wow, you've had quite a—" He stopped himself, certain he'd heard a sound outside. He motioned for them to get down behind their makeshift fort. "I wish you'd gone into the laundry room," he whispered.

"We've been in this together from the start," she whispered back. "Can't get rid of me now."

"If I get the chance, I want to try to talk to—" He stopped again, hearing what sounded like fast-moving footsteps outside. Was someone getting in position to launch an attack?

"We're in here!" Jon yelled loudly. "And we're armed, but we don't want to hurt anyone."

"Release the hostages," a male voice called, "and no one gets hurt."

"We don't know if we can trust you," Jon shouted back. "Who are you?"

"Lieutenant Conrad of the Perpetua Cove Police Department. You can trust me."

"I don't buy that," Jon shouted. "We have good reason to distrust some of the PCPD cops. Tell me why we should trust you!"

When Lieutenant Conrad didn't answer, Jon grew concerned. Was he talking to the enemy? Was this guy involved in Krantz's schemes?

"What do you want?" Lieutenant Conrad yelled. "What are your terms?"

"All I want is to speak to an honest cop," Jon shouted back. "I want someone to listen to our side of the story."

"We already know your side of the story," a second voice shouted. "If you don't send out the hostages right now, we're coming in there! No more game-playing!"

Suddenly what sounded like a disagreement started up outside. Had the second cop overstepped his bounds? Was he perhaps aligned with Krantz? Was this a case of good cop versus bad cop? Jon glanced at Leah, and she looked as puzzled as he felt.

"Do you think Brett or Gordie are out there?" she whispered.

He nodded grimly. "Seems like it." Even so, he was unwilling to give up on Lieutenant Conrad. "I'll tell you my terms," Jon shouted. "There's a note on the back door that explains what's really going on. I want someone trustworthy to get the note and read the facts. Then we can talk."

"We're not falling for that," the second voice shouted. "We know you'll shoot us if we come to the door. Just like you shot Krantz."

"Krantz is a criminal who was trying to kill us. It was self-defense!" Jon yelled.

"Says you!" This was followed by some profanity

and suddenly another argument broke out between the two men.

"Lieutenant Conrad!" Jon tried again. "If you're still there, you need to listen to us. You need to understand that we're the victims here. Officer Krantz tried to kidnap Leah Hampton. I'm an attorney. I tried to reason with Krantz, and he recklessly shot both me and my dog. He's been trying to kill us ever since then. Krantz is a—"

"He shot you because you were fleeing arrest," the other cop yelled. "He was after you because you're criminals!"

"We ran from Krantz because he *didn't* want to arrest us—*he wanted us dead*!" Jon shouted. "We know that Krantz and some of his cop buddies are involved in human trafficking. And drug trafficking, too. Krantz knows we can expose his ring and he can wind up in prison."

"You're the ones doing the trafficking," the voice yelled back. "We've got evidence!"

"That's a lie!" Jon shouted. "You give us the chance and we can prove it. But if you're a friend of Krantz, you probably want us dead, too. That's why you want to storm this house. That's why you're in such a hurry to shoot and kill. You want the girls and Leah's mom dead, too. Because we are all eyewitnesses against Krantz and his buddies." He paused to think. "And we know the names of Erik Krantz's cop buddies, too. *Brett and Gordie.* We don't have last names, but do those names sound familiar? Know anyone by the name of Brett or Gordie?"

This didn't bring an answer and that was troubling. Did that mean he was talking to Brett and Gordie right now? If so, how would they retaliate? And where were the other cops? Were they all crooked? He could hear the sounds of vehement arguing again, but he couldn't make out the words. He and Leah exchanged glances.

The sound of more footsteps, running across the back patio, got Jon's attention. He prepared to shoot the rifle again. But then nothing. Just silence. What was going on out there? Were they getting ready to launch a full attack?

"Lieutenant Conrad!" Jon called out in desperation. For some reason he felt as if this cop might be on the right side—he hoped he was. "Are you still out there?"

"I'm here," a voice yelled back. "Just give yourself up. Come out here so we can talk."

"I wish I could," Jon called back. "But thanks to Krantz and his friends, we know we can't trust just any cop. What's your first name?"

"Michael," he yelled back. "Lieutenant Michael Conrad. I've been on the force for over twenty years. You can trust me. I need to know who told you those names. Who told you that Brett and Gordie couldn't be trusted?"

"The girls we rescued. The ones that Krantz kidnapped and held in that filthy warehouse," Jon yelled back, deciding that if no one was going to read his note, he'd just have to shout out as much of their story as possible. Someone had to hear it! "Hallie and Rosita told us about Brett and Gordie. The girls said they're the other policemen working with Krantz. All three

CPPD cops and another man—possibly more—are involved in human trafficking. According to the girls your cops are moving drugs, too." He paused to catch his breath, waiting to see if Lieutenant Conrad responded. When he didn't, Jon continued, talking fast and loud and hoping—praying—someone was really listening.

"The girls were supposed to get picked up by boat tonight. A guy called Mack is involved with that—he's probably out on the ocean right now. And Krantz was trying to get the girls and Leah's mother out of the warehouse and onto the boat. The reason I shot Krantz was to protect those girls and Leah's mother. And to protect ourselves. It's all in my note."

"And I've sent out a text message," Leah shouted suddenly. "I sent all this information out to the state police, FBI and the coast guard. Real help is on the way!"

Jon wasn't sure this information would be helpful, but there was nothing he could do about it now. There was another long silence, and Jon wasn't sure if this was a good sign or a bad one.

"Lieutenant Conrad?" he yelled. "Are you still listening?"

"I sure hope Brett and Gordie aren't out there listening," Leah whispered. "That could—"

A noise from behind made them both turn around. "Someone's trying to break in through the front door." Leah pointed a shaky revolver toward the front of the house.

"Lieutenant Conrad!" Jon yelled again. "I thought we were talking. Why are your guys busting down the front door?"

If Lieutenant Conrad answered, Jon couldn't hear him because of the pounding on the door. "Get into the laundry room," Jon said in no uncertain terms. "Now!" He was off the stool, pushing her toward the laundry room, determined to get her out of what could turn into a bloodbath. "*I mean it.* Take care of your mom and the girls."

"I can't—"

"Now!" He shoved her toward the door. *"Run!"*

To his relief, she obeyed and just as she closed the laundry room door, the front door burst open and he ducked down into the fort.

"Get your hands up in the air! *Now!*" This command came from the front of the house and sounded like the same cop who'd been arguing with Lieutenant Conrad. "I'm counting to three and then I'll open fire—"

"I want to talk to an honest cop *right now*! And not anyone—" His words were cut off by the sound of the back door being kicked open and suddenly gunfire broke out from what felt like every direction. Knowing he couldn't fight this many automatic weapons, Jon hit the floor in the makeshift fort and, wrapping his hands around his head, he prepared to meet his Maker.

Leah huddled with the girls and her mother beside the washing machine, tucked in the far corner of the laundry room. Wrapping her arms around the three of them, she listened in horror as round after round of shots rang in the house. Her blood ran cold as she imagined Jon completely surrounded by lawless lawmen, wounded, bleeding. No way could he survive that much gunfire. No one could. And then, as quickly as it began, it seemed to be over.

Numb with fear and dread, she listened to the sounds of shouting and scuffling just outside the laundry room door. She couldn't make out the words, but people were clearly angry. And then there were two more shots, followed by a brief silence—and then more agitated voices.

"God help us," Leah prayed quietly in a trembling voice. "Please, protect Hallie and Rosita and my mom. Don't let anyone hurt them." Her prayer was interrupted by more yelling and scuffling. The words were unintelligible, but there was definitely a disagreement going on. Was Jon still putting up a fight? Still alive? She strained her ears, longing to hear Jon's voice in the mix.

"What's happening?" Hallie asked.

"I don't know," Leah whispered. "But I need to get rid of this." She pulled the revolver from her pocket, then slipped it behind the washing machine, sliding it way back against the wall and beneath the machine. "I don't want to give anyone an excuse to have a shoot-out with us." She slowly stood, knowing it was just a matter of time before they were discovered in the laundry room. She needed to do whatever she could to spare the girls and her mom. Even if that meant they would shoot her, too. It was their only hope.

"I'm coming out!" she yelled loudly as she reached for the laundry room doorknob. "I'm unarmed. Don't shoot!"

"Come out with your hands up," a loud voice yelled.

"Is Lieutenant Conrad there?" Leah asked from behind the door. "I'd feel safer if he was there."

"I'm here!" he shouted. "Come out now. Hands high in the air. Move slowly."

Bracing herself, Leah cracked open the door, cautiously stepping into the kitchen with her hands held high. As she saw firearms aimed in her direction, she knew this might be a trick, but she also knew she was out of options.

"I'm Leah Hampton," she announced as she came out. Someone had turned a light on in the kitchen, and she could see that the room was filled with law enforcement officers, many of them in riot gear and all wielding firearms. "I contacted the state police and FBI and coast guard, and told them the truth," she said quickly. "That Jon Wilson and I are both innocent—that Krantz and his buddies are trying to frame us and—" Before she could finish her sentence, a uniformed female officer came over and, with a gun in hand, told Leah to slowly lower her hands and place them behind her back.

"But I'm innocent."

"Just do it," the woman said firmly.

Leah did as she was told.

"It's procedural," the woman said in a quiet voice as she cuffed Leah's hands. "For your safety as much as for ours."

"Oh…?" Leah glanced around the room. "Where's Jon?"

"They took him outside."

"Is he—?"

"He's on his way to the hospital." The woman peered closely at Leah. "Do you need medical attention?"

"I'm not sure." Leah frowned at the dark uniform, then at the woman's face. *"Who are you?"*

"I'm Detective Brianna Crawley, Oregon State Police."

Leah's eyes filled with relieved tears. *"Really?* The state police got my message? *You came?"*

"Just in time, it seems."

After ensuring that her mother was safely back in her room at The Willows and discovering that Jon had been admitted to the hospital for treatment of his original gunshot wound in the leg, Leah spent the rest of the evening in the Cape Perpetua police station being interviewed by Detective Crawley. Glad to spill the whole strange story, Leah made a full statement and answered all the detective's questions.

When it was time to go home, Leah was pleasantly surprised that Lieutenant Conrad met her in the reception area with a little brown dog in his arms. Leah eagerly reached for Ralph, thankful that he seemed just fine. As the lieutenant walked her out to her car, he reassured her that, aside from Krantz and his cohorts, who were in custody, the rest of the police force in Cape Perpetua was completely trustworthy. "You should be completely secure, but just to be safe we'll keep officers posted near your home. Call us if you have any concerns."

By the time Leah fell into her own bed, she was too exhausted to think clearly, but there was still one unanswered question rumbling around in her head. That was regarding Jon. Was there really something between them—did he have the same strong feelings she'd been experiencing? Or had their relationship been temporary—just the result of being forced together by a dire situation? All she could do was pray about it and fall into a deep and much-needed slumber.

NINETEEN

In the morning, Leah felt like a new woman. And upon examining Ralph's gunshot wound, she was relieved to see that he was nearly healed up. After they both enjoyed a hearty breakfast, she walked over to the hospital to check on Jon and to return his phone, which was now dead. To her surprise, he was already released and the nurse in charge explained that a friend had picked him up and transported him back to his home in Portland.

As she drove back home, Leah tried not to feel too let down. It actually made sense that Jon would want to return to Portland where he could visit his own doctor and relax in his own home. And because she still had Jon's phone and his mother's dog, she knew that he would have to be in touch…eventually. But she did feel somewhat cut-off and set adrift, being away from him like this. Still, with school and work, she had plenty to do. And fortunately, her great-aunt was happy to care for Ralph during the day.

By the time the weekend was approaching, Leah was feeling uneasy. Surely Jon hadn't forgotten about her—and even if he had, would he forget about his mom's dog? She was just leaving The Willows after finishing her shift on Friday afternoon when Marsha in the reception area stopped her, explaining that a guy named Jon had just called. "He asked you to bring his dog to the beach house."

Leah thanked her and, feeling a mixture of excitement and anxiety, hurried home to gather up Ralph before heading over to the beach. She hadn't been out that way since their ordeal and wasn't sure she was ready for it now—or maybe she wasn't ready to see Jon and have him treat her like a casual acquaintance. Because that was how she'd decided it was probably going to end. Guys like Jon Wilson didn't fall for girls like her. For all Leah knew, the "friend" who'd picked up Jon from the hospital might've been the beautiful Monica. Perhaps she'd heard about his brush with death and come running to his side. Why not?

Bracing herself for whatever was coming, Leah knocked on the door. To her surprise it was jerked open and Jon, wearing a huge grin and using a cane, rushed toward her. He hugged her for a long delightful moment, finally giving her a long intense kiss that shot shivers of happiness through her. "Do you know how much I missed you?" he asked her as he reached for Ralph. He gave the pup a playful tousle as he placed him on the floor, then stood back up to look at Leah. "You're even more beautiful than I remembered."

"Thank you." She just stared at him, unsure of what to say. "I missed you, too. I didn't know how to reach you." She produced his phone.

"Me, too. I tried calling this." He pocketed his phone. "But it was off."

"Dead," she explained.

"Aha." He pointed to his bandaged leg. "I had to have some surgery. No big deal, but I was supposed to stay put a few days." He grinned with a twinkle in his eyes. "And I put that downtime to good use." He grabbed her hand, hobbling along. "Come see." He led her to a room in the back of the house that looked out over the ocean.

"What a stunning view," she said as she stared out the large window. "I never saw it before because the drapes were closed."

"And it's good light in here, too—great for painting." He reached for her hand, turning her away from the window. "This is what I want you to see, Leah." He led her to an easel that was draped in a faded blue sheet. With a flourish, he removed it, and to her astonishment, she was staring at her own face—only it seemed much more beautiful.

In the portrait, her honey-colored hair was loose and radiant, flowing in the breeze. Her skin was smooth and golden, luminous. Her eyes were bright and clear, the same color as the ocean behind her, and the whole thing was washed in amazing sunlight that made it seem alive somehow.

"Wow." She went closer to see the painting better. If a picture was worth a thousand words, a portrait should be worth a million. Because, unless she was mistaken, Jon was in love with her. Much more so than he'd ever been with Monica. She knew it!

"It's not as beautiful as you are," he apologized. "But for my first attempt, it's not half-bad. Especially when you consider I was working from news media photos and my memory." He gathered her in his arms again. "I'm hoping that you'll let me do another portrait, Leah. From real life." He kissed her again. "I'd like to do a lot of portraits of you. Some on our milestone anniversaries, some with our children, some as we grow old together. Do you think you would mind?"

She couldn't stop her tears as she hugged him again, burying her head into his chest. "I wouldn't mind at all, Jon. In fact, it would make me very, very happy."

"Not as happy as you make me. I love you, Leah. I want to spend the rest of my days with you—I really do! I think I started falling for you that first time we met on the beach. Remember that day when Ralph brought us together?"

She nodded eagerly. "I do."

"Well, I knew he'd gotten it right. And that's why we'd been out looking for you. I wanted a proper introduction."

"Well, I guess you got that." She made a nervous laugh, trying to take all this in—telling herself this was not just a dream.

He leaned down to kiss her once more, lingering so long that she felt herself being swept away like a warm summer tide—beautifully swept away.

"So what do you think of all this?" he asked as he stroked her cheek.

She smiled up at him with a heart so full she was almost afraid to breathe. "I love you, too, Jon. For a while I tried to convince myself that I was wrong, but my heart wouldn't let me."

"I'm so thankful."

"And I'm thankful that Ralph chased me that day," she told him. "That he brought us together."

"And he led me to you when you were in danger, too."

"Do we get to keep him?" she asked quietly.

Jon just laughed…then eagerly nodded. "If you want Ralph, Leah, he's all yours. Along with me!"

One year later

Leah Hampton and Jon Wilson celebrated their love by reciting their marriage vows today. Their wedding was held on the very same beach they'd met on one year ago.

Among the wedding guests of family and friends and several uniformed Cape Perpetua police officers were seven grateful young women. These girls were rescued when Jon and Leah exposed the human trafficking ring that had plagued the Cape Perpetua region for a few years.

Also in attendance at the wedding was the family dog, named Ralph, who performed the service of ring bearer.

After a honeymoon in Maui, the newlywed couple and Ralph will reside in the Wilson beach cabin, where the groom will paint and practice criminal law and the bride will work as a registered nurse at a local nursing home.

* * * * *

COMING NEXT MONTH FROM
Love Inspired® Suspense

Available April 5, 2016

PROTECT AND SERVE
Rookie K-9 Unit • by Terri Reed
When dog trainer Gina Perry's boss is murdered and the killer comes after her, she must rely on rookie officer Shane West and his K-9 partner to keep her alive. But can she protect her heart?

MIRROR IMAGE
SWAT: Top Cops • by Laura Scott
Sheriff's deputy Jenna Reed thought she was an only child—until an attacker mistook her for the sister she didn't know existed. Now she needs help from her boss, Lieutenant Griff Vaughn, if she hopes to bring down the human trafficking ring her long-lost sister escaped from.

TAILSPIN
Mountain Cove • by Elizabeth Goddard
Bush pilot Will Pierson and scuba diver Sylvie Masters are determined to find the cause of the seaplane crash that killed both their mothers. But someone will do anything to keep the truth from surfacing.

CODE OF SILENCE • by Heather Woodhaven
Gabriella Radcliffe's late mother stole evidence of criminal activity from the Mafia, and now Gabriella has twenty-four hours to find it—or her aunt will die. With Luke McGuire's help, can she make the deadline?

REUNION MISSION
Rangers Under Fire • by Virginia Vaughan
When DEA agent Matt Ross returns to his hometown on a case, he discovers his high school sweetheart, Claire Kendall, standing over his informant's dead body. Afraid that she's in danger—and being framed—Matt vows to find the killer.

PICTURE PERFECT MURDER • by Rachel Dylan
Former CIA agent Lily Parker escapes a serial killer's clutches, but he's determined to finish the job. So she turns to FBI agent Rex Sullivan for help outwitting the obsessed criminal.

LISCNM0316

REQUEST YOUR FREE BOOKS!

2 FREE RIVETING INSPIRATIONAL NOVELS
PLUS 2 FREE MYSTERY GIFTS

Love Inspired®
SUSPENSE
RIVETING INSPIRATIONAL ROMANCE

YES! Please send me 2 FREE Love Inspired® Suspense novels and my 2 FREE mystery gifts (gifts are worth about $10). After receiving them, if I don't wish to receive any more books, I can return the shipping statement marked "cancel." If I don't cancel, I will receive 4 brand-new novels every month and be billed just $4.99 per book in the U.S. or $5.49 per book in Canada. That's a savings of at least 17% off the cover price. It's quite a bargain! Shipping and handling is just 50¢ per book in the U.S. and 75¢ per book in Canada.* I understand that accepting the 2 free books and gifts places me under no obligation to buy anything. I can always return a shipment and cancel at any time. Even if I never buy another book, the two free books and gifts are mine to keep forever.

123/323 IDN GH5Z

Name _____ (PLEASE PRINT) _____

Address _____ Apt. # _____

City _____ State/Prov. _____ Zip/Postal Code _____

Signature (if under 18, a parent or guardian must sign) _____

Mail to the **Reader Service:**
IN U.S.A.: P.O. Box 1867, Buffalo, NY 14240-1867
IN CANADA: P.O. Box 609, Fort Erie, Ontario L2A 5X3

**Are you a current subscriber to Love Inspired® Suspense books
and want to receive the larger-print edition?
Call 1-800-873-8635 or visit www.ReaderService.com.**

* Terms and prices subject to change without notice. Prices do not include applicable taxes. Sales tax applicable in N.Y. Canadian residents will be charged applicable taxes. Offer not valid in Quebec. This offer is limited to one order per household. Not valid for current subscribers to Love Inspired Suspense books. All orders subject to credit approval. Credit or debit balances in a customer's account(s) may be offset by any other outstanding balance owed by or to the customer. Please allow 4 to 6 weeks for delivery. Offer available while quantities last.

Your Privacy—The Reader Service is committed to protecting your privacy. Our Privacy Policy is available online at www.ReaderService.com or upon request from the Reader Service.
We make a portion of our mailing list available to reputable third parties that offer products we believe may interest you. If you prefer that we not exchange your name with third parties, or if you wish to clarify or modify your communication preferences, please visit us at www.ReaderService.com/consumerschoice or write to us at Reader Service Preference Service, P.O. Box 9062, Buffalo, NY 14240-9062. Include your complete name and address.

LIS15

Turn your love of reading into
rewards you'll love with
Harlequin My Rewards

**Join for FREE today at
www.HarlequinMyRewards.com**

Earn **FREE BOOKS** of your choice.

Experience **EXCLUSIVE OFFERS** and contests.

Enjoy **BOOK RECOMMENDATIONS**
selected just for you.

PLUS! Sign up now
and get **500** points
right away!

MYR16R